PRAISE FOR STARWEBS INC.

(Originally Published as *A Manhattan Ghost Story – A Christmas Carol Revisited*)

"Did you hear the applause in the middle of the Welsh night! We did! Attention was paid to your singular contribution to tonight's Program. . . a very poignant and powerful script."
(Frances Scanlon - Secretary of the New York City Bar Association Entertainment Committee - A staged adaptation of this reworking of the well-loved Christmas ghost story was performed in Manhattan on December 19th, 2012, at the House of the Bar for a charity event to celebrate the 200th anniversary of Dickens' birth.)

"I thought it was very, very, good indeed. . . Phil put a new twist to it. It was great. . . He's got some great imagery. . . fantastic. . . I loved it! I like the way the story unfolded. . . What Phil's done is taken a very pertinent subject, Timaeus, 'Of the Time'. . . Ebenezer Clinton Scrooge III, what a great character to base a novel around!"
(Nigel Crowle – Author – 'Roy's Read's' BBC Radio Wales 21st November 2011)

"What a wonderful message to remind ourselves of, and to remind others of. . . It's just beautiful. . . They adopted 'because'. . . I don't want to ruin the story for new readers. I love it."
(Michele Vrabel - U.S.)

"The vibrant prose style of the author holds the reader's interest and draws one into the tale. The harmonics between the Dickens tale and the Manhattan story enhance the reading experience as they unfold and are noted in the plot. The whole concept devised by the author is quite brilliant."
(Leonard Shurey - Wales, U.K.)

"A great read. Brilliant up to date version of a Christmas Carol. Really makes you think."
(T. L. Jones - U.K.)

"I loved it!!!"
(Paivi Lokard - Sweden)

"If you loved Dickens' 'Christmas Carol' you'll love this book."
(KnownAsJane – U.S.)

"No faint-hearted writer this! He plunges right in, adapting the story to present day America, but more importantly, a very claustrophobic America of soaring structures and crowded walkways. Before I even had the chance to wonder how he was ever going to pull off a remake of one of my favourite author's works he had me immersed in this crowded yet lonely place, following his protagonist as one by one he introduces mysteries one cannot help but think will be revisited as the night goes on. . . This story is truly amazing. . . the imagery at Phil's command is VERY IMPRESSIVE. Great stuff!!
By the time he has finished, Phil Rowlands has proved himself the Master of Imagery. I felt as if I were in a dream. . . a psychedelic rush. . . with light and colour hitting me from all directions. . . this story is quite a trip. . . . this author is a real talent to watch."
(John W. Cassell – Author of *CROSSROADS:1969*)

Starwebs Inc.

Phil Rowlands

DEDICATION

A Humble Tribute to A Great Man and Social Commentator

Charles Dickens 1812 - 1870

ACKNOWLEDGMENTS

With special thanks to Family and Friends for their constant encouragement.

"Praise is like sunlight to the human spirit: we cannot flower and grow without it."
Jess Lair

DISCLAIMER
"Starwebs Inc. **is a work of fiction; therefore, the novel's story and characters are fictitious.** Any public agencies, institutions, or historical figures mentioned in the story serve as a backdrop to the characters and their actions, which are wholly imaginary.

CONTENTS

Through tinted windows, Ebenezer Clinton Scrooge III watched the bustling sidewalk crowds slip silently into the waiting night, shadowy grey wraiths spirited away on a bitter December wind. The gaudy festive lights served only to emphasise their desperate anonymity. Scrooge leaned back into the plush leather upholstery of the limousine, comforted by the fact he no longer needed to mingle with the madding crowd.

"Far from the madding crowd's ignoble strife. . ." mused Scrooge. His train of thought was interrupted by Grainger, his chauffeur.

"What crazy crowd you looking to avoid, Mr Scrooge?"

It's a quote from a poem, Grainger. The writer is referring to the common herd of humanity, God help them. Don't worry about it, man, just drive.

Scrooge glanced impatiently at his watch, then out of the window.

It was as the car slowed at the intersection of 52nd Street that he thought he saw 'the face'. Someone was standing on the sidewalk, staring directly at him, which was impossible because, from the outside, the windows presented an impenetrable black veil. Someone, the bubbling froth of humanity, flowed around like water in a rushing stream as it broke over an ancient, immovable stone. Someone with eyes exactly like, no, that could not be! For an instant, the chill night air embraced him, rendering impotent the luxurious, heated interior of the imported Bentley. He leaned forward, striking his face sharply against the glass, in a futile attempt to confirm or, more likely, disprove his initial impression. The figure was no longer there.

"Goddamit! Pull over Grainger, now!" he ordered.

"Everything ok, sir?" inquired Grainger.

"Do it, man!" barked Scrooge.

With a squeal of brakes, the limousine pulled over sharply amid blaring horns as traffic swerved to avoid making costly contact. Startled shoppers edged away from the kerb and hurried on their way, except for one who watched Scrooge stumble out of the car.

The individual smiled as Scrooge desperately searched the faces in the bustling sidewalk crowds. At last, Scrooge's gaze fixed upon him, recognition widening his eyes. Scrooge staggered back. Satisfied it had been recognised, the figure turned up its collar and melted away into the night.

"No, impossible," muttered Scrooge.

"You Ok, Mr Scrooge?" inquired a concerned Grainger as he ushered Scrooge back into the safety of the car, closing the door firmly behind him. Puzzled, he swept his immediate surroundings for anything that might explain his employer's strange behaviour. He saw nothing. Deciding that the best course of action was to put distance between Scrooge and whatever had unsettled him, he climbed back into the driver's seat.

In the mirror, he could see Scrooge's head sunk back in the upholstery, beads of perspiration trickling down his cheeks like silent tears.

"Did you see him, Grainger?" Grainger was about to start the car, but Scrooge's words caused him to pause and look out the window.

"See who, Mr Scrooge?" he asked, curious as to who could have spooked the normally unflappable Ebenezer Clinton Scrooge III.

"The guy standing by the drug store."

Grainger glanced back up at the mirror. Scrooge was running his tongue over dry lips.

"There were a lot of guys by the drug store, Mr Scrooge, does yours have a name?"

"Jake Marley."

Grainger's eyes narrowed, betraying his concern.

"Mr Marley? But Mr Marley's dead, sir, has been for some time."

"Really? Must have slipped my mind. I know he's dead, you idiot, but don't they say everyone has a double?"

"Not Mr Marley, sir, he was real unique."

"He was that, alright," retorted Scrooge as he closed his eyes. His thoughts drifted back many years, just after he and Jake had joined the company.

Manhattan, Christmas Eve 1989.
Scrooge is seated at a desk, shuffling a pile of papers into his briefcase. He looks up as the door opens and Jake Marley enters. The unwelcome sounds of music and laughter drift into the room; the office party is in full swing.

Jake stands by the door, a glass of wine in his hand and a paper party hat askew on his head. He is clearly intoxicated and intent on making his usual spectacle of himself. He weaves his way unsteadily to Scrooge's desk and perches on one end. From behind his back, he produces a bunch of mistletoe.

"So, this is where you've been hiding, Ebenezer?"

Scrooge continues stuffing papers into his briefcase and does not attempt to reply.

"Saved you some mistletoe," continued Jake, undeterred, "seemed a shame to waste it. Lots of lonely hot temps out there."

"I'm a married man now, Jake," replied Scrooge, not looking up, "guess that must have slipped your mind."

"As if," said Jake, taking a sip of wine, "how is the lovely Valarie?"

Scrooge ignored the question and began fastening his briefcase.

"What are you up to this Christmas, Ebenezer? How about you and Val spending it over at my place? There's plenty of room for a few more old friends."

Scrooge placed the upright briefcase between him and Jake.

"Thank you, no. We like a quiet Christmas."

"You mean you do, as far as I can recall, Val was always up for a good party."

Scrooge stood and looked Jake in the eye.

"She's in no condition to party."

"Not pregnant, is she?" inquired Jake, "Ebenezer, you old dog!"

"She's unwell," said Scrooge, his words as cold as December sleet, "now if you'll excuse me."

He moved away from the desk and walked towards the door, but Jake's words brought him up short.

"So that's what they call it these days. You make sure you take good care of that girl. I'm still sore you beat me to the punch."

Scrooge half turned to face Jake.

"I told you, she's sick. We're not ready for kids just yet."

Scrooge is about to turn his back on Jake and walk towards the door, but Jake's question forces a terse response.

"What about Leah? What's her boy called again?"

Scrooge knew Jake had not forgotten, but he had to say the name.

"Stephen."

"Stephen, huh? He must be about six or seven now. Bet he's real excited. Christmas is all about kids. You going to be taking his present over on the day?"

"No, it's being delivered."

"Delivered? Right!

Scrooge felt the contempt that punctuates Jake's words like a slap.

The door opens, and Scrooge is saved the indignity of having to respond. A stunning young brunette in a tight party dress sporting a deep cleavage leans against the door frame. She smiles provocatively at Jake.

"Come on, Jake honey, you're missing all the fun," she said, assuming a fake pout.

"Be right there, baby," replied Jake, downing the remains of his glass. Her eyes alight on Scrooge, giving him a quick once-over. The smile that was about to break on her lips fades rapidly as she encounters Scrooge's grim expression. Jake crosses the room and puts an arm around her waist. He turned to Scrooge and raised his empty glass.

"You have a good one, then Ebenezer. Don't forget to give my love to that beautiful wife of yours."

The door slams shut behind them.

Scrooge opened his eyes and sighed with relief. It was hot inside the limousine. He took out a silk handkerchief and began to mop his brow.

"Seems kinda a shame you and Mr Marley never spoke for a long time before his accident. 'Life's too short to quarrel over', as my old Pappy used to say."

Grainger's disembodied words over the intercom were an unwelcome intrusion.

"Then your old Pappy was a fool! Guess that's why he died poor. Now mind the business I pay you for, or you may end up following in Pappy's footsteps."

Ahead, the congestion eased slightly, and the limousine moved on with menacing grace through the swirling rush-hour traffic.

A simple trick of the light—that was all. Besides, they say everyone has a double. Still, there had been no mistaking the irascible gleam that always warned Scrooge that his old partner and adversary had precisely gauged the subtle machinations of his devious mind.

Strange, it was a sensation that momentarily overwhelmed him with nostalgia. He was not a sentimental man, far from it, but he missed the challenge of an equal. In the days and years following 'the accident', there had been no one of sufficient intellect and force of character to hinder Scrooge's ruthless march to power. Control the media and you control the masses.

He smiled at the thought that while the world was, to all intents and purposes, unaware of his existence, he could at will delve into men's minds and plant seeds that took root, grew, and bore very profitable fruit indeed. That was what caused the rift, and with each passing day, it widened until a yawning chasm opened between them that nothing on this earth could bridge.

It was not that either man was opposed to using manipulation as a perfectly acceptable way of influencing the thoughts and opinions of the vast global audience the company had amassed through its satellite, television, and media empire. Mind control via channels like subliminal messaging was a widely accepted marketing method employed by all the major corporations, whether they wanted someone to buy a particular brand of toilet roll or drag a nation into war.

Despite himself, his thoughts drifted back.

The Board Room, Manhattan 1993

Eager board members surround Scrooge. One by one, they shake his hand and pat him on the back before departing. Only one member shows less enthusiasm. Jake Marley remains seated, arms behind his head, feet resting on the polished mahogany table.

As soon as they are alone, Jake sits upright and leans forward.

"We need to talk," announced Jake.

Scrooge remained standing.

"What now, Jake?"

"You know what! This proposed contract of yours."

Jake is obviously struggling to suppress his feelings.

"You mean the most lucrative contract this company has ever secured in its entire history? The contract that will elevate us to another level?"

Scrooge believes his position is unassailable.

"Not just another level, Ebenezer; another ballpark. The political ramifications are immense. Have you truly considered where this deal might lead us?"

Jake is pushing hard, but Scrooge sidesteps the question. It is irrelevant now.

"I'm a businessman, Jake, not a politician."

"So was Michael Corleone!"

Scrooge almost smiled at the comparison.

"Slightly melodramatic even by your standards, Jake. You made your pitch, I swear I could feel the fire and smell the brimstone, but the board went with me. Deal with it. You always were a sore loser."

The conversation was not merely over; it was redundant. Scrooge turned his back on Jake and made to leave.

"You're a very persuasive guy, Ebenezer. Val discovered that to her cost."

Scrooge turned back sharply, his features contorted with anger.

"What did you just say?"

"Sorry, maybe I shouldn't have crossed that particular line," responded Jake with obvious reluctance, "but we both know if this deal goes through, it could plunge a nation into war."

"Goodbye, Jake," said Scrooge, turning away.

'Plunge a nation into war!' crackled a voice over the intercom.

"What?" muttered a startled Scrooge.

Beads of perspiration merged and trickled in tiny rivulets down Scrooge's jowls. As he dabbed at them, the source of his sudden unease burst through the surface of his consciousness like a drowning man's last desperate gasp for air. They were words once uttered accusingly at him with a vehemence that had momentarily left him speechless. Words that had severed the final frayed bond of friendship forever. Jake's words.

"It's almost Time, Ebenezer."

The sudden disruption of his reverie by a disembodied voice on the car's internal intercom had unsettled him badly. He pressed a button and established communication with Grainger, his Chauffeur.

"What did you say, Grainger?"

Although even as he spoke, he knew the answer. Grainger would not dare to be so familiar. It had not been Grainger's voice he had heard.

"Nothing, sir, at least not just then, but I have been trying to speak with you for the last ten minutes. The intercom must be playing up."

"It would be easier to waken the dead!"

"Pardon!"

Scrooge swallowed hard. His throat had become unusually constricted.

"I said the intercom must be playing up, sir. Seems as if we have a few gremlins in our systems tonight. Apparently, the lift to your private car park is jammed. We'll have to stop outside and use the main entrance."

"With the common herd!"

That voice again. Not Grainger's, but another he knew all too well. Leaning forward, he peered over Grainger's unsuspecting shoulders into the mirror above his chauffeur's head. Dark brown eyes stared back at him; eyes that could not be Grainger's because his were blue. The eyes blinked, and they were blue again.

Scrooge continued to dab at his brow with the silken handkerchief. It was oppressively warm; perhaps gremlins had also managed to disrupt the air conditioning.

His head began to throb. Whether it was a direct result of him hitting it against the reinforced glass or the sudden unwelcome realisation that he did not want Grainger to turn around because he was no longer sure that the person sitting directly in front of him was Grainger.

This was absurd!

The car pulled up in front of the monstrous edifice that Scrooge recognised at once as home. He exhaled, and the tension flooded out of him. Get a grip! What on earth had come over him? A vaguely familiar face in the crowd, and his imagination had gone off on one Big Time, to quote the vernacular, something he normally avoided at all costs.

He sank back into the welcoming folds of the padded interior as the car slowed gently to a stop.

Though usually impervious to the pressures that oppress powerful men, he had to admit to himself that the recent clandestine 'arrangement' made with certain shadowy emissaries of State had stirred in him the first spasms of anxiety since, well, a long time.

After Watergate, no one could be considered immune, and what if this new 'venture' was a bridge too far? It was too late now; the die had been cast, and besides, the potential pay-off was immense.

"Here we are, sir."

"Final Destination."

The words jolted Scrooge back into the present, scattering his thoughts like a flock of startled crows. 'Final Destination' evoked morbid images of hapless teenagers meeting untimely ends in a variety of ingenious and gruesome ways. Not that he was particularly opposed to the idea of such a fate befalling a sizeable portion of the youthful population.

What use were most of them anyway? Drugs and sex seemed to be the only activities they pursued with any enthusiasm. The language they spoke was, by and large, totally incomprehensible. Unless they enlisted in the armed forces, where their energies could be channelled and directed towards more constructive purposes, Scrooge saw little to justify their aimless existence.

A sharp rap on his window jolted Scrooge out of his reverie. A distorted face pressed against the tinted glass. A face framed by an unkempt, greasy beard peered blindly at him.

"Sit tight, Mr Scrooge," urged Grainger, "I'll sort it."

Grainger opened the driver's door, and Scrooge watched his large bulk disappear onto the sidewalk with a growing apprehension that he was unable to exorcise. Normally, Grainger's presence was a source of reassurance, offering protection and exuding intimidation in equal measure. No, Caesar felt more secure surrounded by his Praetorian Guard than Scrooge felt with the massive figure of Grainger at his side. But not today.

An ominous sense of foreboding seeped like fog into the interior of the limousine, and he was a child again hiding under his bed while the familiar dread footfalls ascended the staircase before halting deliberately outside his bedroom door. The silence was always the worst, holding within itself all the pregnant possibilities of a child's fear.

Silhouetted against the smoked glass, Grainger appeared somehow much smaller and infinitely more menacing as he removed the hapless intruder. Scrooge watched as Grainger manhandled the vagrant away from the car.

Obeying a primal instinct, Scrooge hurried to secure the internal lock just as someone tried to open the door from outside. How many times had Grainger performed this same procedure, shielding his master from any possible unwanted media attention with his huge frame, as Scrooge emerged warily from his black cocoon? Thousands probably. But today was different, and this could not be Grainger. Security, perhaps?

The door was being pulled open from the outside with irresistible force. There was no bed to cower under, so Scrooge eased himself out into the grey December twilight.

No one was there. Where was Grainger? If Security hadn't opened the door, then who had? Scrooge remained with his back to the limousine, reluctant to abandon the potential sanctuary it might still offer.

Then he saw Grainger.

He was about twenty yards away, seemingly engaged in a one-sided wrestling match with some unfortunate individual who now lay pinned to the floor but was clearly not yet fully subdued.

Scrooge surveyed the immediate area with growing alarm. Could there be more than one attacker? He knew that the latest project he had agreed to pursue was not without risk, but had not anticipated that risk to be of a physical kind. Certainly not as crude as an attack on the street in broad daylight. And where was Security? Surely, they would have been waiting for him to arrive once they knew the private lift had broken down. Something was very wrong.

Prevarication had never been one of Scrooge's vices. After assessing the situation, he swiftly determined a course of action. Taking refuge in the limousine, although tempting, was not a sensible option. Determined individuals bold enough to perpetrate an assault on the very steps of the citadel of his personal empire would not be deterred by a locked door.

Clearly, 'they' had succeeded in disrupting communications between the limousine and his supposedly secure channel at 'Starwebs Inc.', which explains the absence of Security and senior staff members. It also suggests that whoever planned this had access to some highly advanced hardware indeed.

There were no signs of angels or demons on the marble steps, which rose like Jacob's ladder from the frozen sidewalk. He was alone and vulnerable, waiting for darkness to fall and the call of the Bogeyman.

To his left, Grainger seemed to have the situation entirely under control, but why was he marching the unfortunate individual towards Scrooge and not away from him?

Wasn't Caesar murdered by those he trusted most?

Shadowy figures were beginning to descend the marble steps towards them.

Security had evidently finally got its act together. He glanced at Grainger, who had stopped a few feet away with the unfortunate individual firmly and painfully in his grip. Scrooge decided to err on the side of caution. Leaving the individual in Grainger's tender care, he turned to ascend the steps of his citadel.

Two steps up, he paused. Something felt slightly wrong. The figures on the steps were still moving towards him, but very slowly. In fact, they moved in unison, keeping pace with each other as they carried a heavy oak coffin, like the bearers he had once watched following a funeral cortège.

He remembered it as if it were yesterday. It had been Jacob's funeral. He stepped back and blinked.

When he opened his eyes, they had vanished.

Grainger still stood several feet away, holding a scruffy individual who had now ceased struggling and accepted the inevitable. His face was almost hidden beneath long, greasy strands of what Scrooge believed must once have been blond hair. His beard was matted and covered a mass of ugly scars that dragged the skin around his eye down towards his disfigured cheek.

Scrooge noted with some distaste that he was missing a left forearm.

He smiled. This was no hired assassin sent on a mission to destroy only a common beggar chancing his arm, or what remained of it. A diseased symptom of the times. New York was infested with such hopeless souls seeking solace and oblivion in alcohol or drugs, authors of their own destruction, and as such deserving of no sympathy or special favours.

Still, they never usually surfaced in this district, preferring instead to haunt the more stagnant cesspits of the city. Perhaps the fact that it was Christmas Eve emboldened this particular specimen into venturing further afield in the false hope that honest citizens would be more inclined to lunatic displays of charity, many being so imbued with festive spirits that they would carelessly part with their hard-earned dollars.

The man had the audacity to stare brazenly at Scrooge as if he were his equal. Why hadn't Grainger simply sent him packing? Attuned through many years of service to his master's needs, Grainger responded swiftly.

"My God!" muttered Scrooge, appalled by the spectacle. "From what gutter did he crawl out of?"

"I would have sent him on his way, sir, but he says he knows you," explained Grainger.

"Have you completely lost it, man? Does he look remotely like someone who moves in the same social circles?"

Scrooge was outraged. But even as he uttered the words, awareness rose like an unsettling mist from some dark subterranean reservoir of his mind that somewhere in a previous existence, he had crossed paths with this wretched creature.

He extinguished the thought as easily as a lit candle.

"Well, what do you want?" he inquired roughly.

Suddenly aware of his plight, the beggar averted his eyes, now dark and heavy as if their light had also dimmed.

"I thought."

"I know what you thought." Scrooge's every word oozed with contempt. "The same your sort always thinks. Why did you come here?"

"I have a message for Mr Ebenezer Scrooge," the vagrant replied.

"A message for me," sneered Scrooge. "Who sent you?"

"A mutual friend," mumbled the creature.

"Mutual, really, well, spit it out," commanded Scrooge, beginning to find the conversation, such as it was, tiresome.

"Merry Christmas," proclaimed the vagrant.

It sounded more like the casting of a curse than the giving of a blessing.

"Excuse me?"

Scrooge hesitated, unsure whether he had heard correctly. To his astonishment, the creature lifted its head, and eyes that were no longer cowed held Scrooge's scornful gaze until he was almost compelled to look away.

"I said, Merry Christmas, Ebenezer."

The stranger spoke the words with slow deliberation, as if he were sitting in judgment and passing sentence on a man found guilty of a heinous crime.

Anger flooded through Scrooge, rendering him momentarily speechless and causing his hands to clench into tight fists. He stepped forward, one hand raised above his head, ready to deliver the blow that his powerless tongue could not utter.

"How dare you!"

"Leave this to us, sir."

Large, ominous shapes brushed past Scrooge and seized the unfortunate individual who had dared to carry the pungent odour of failure and despair to the very steps of this towering capitalist monument, they had been chosen to defend.

Security had finally arrived, and not a moment too soon.

In truth, Scrooge felt a great relief; physical violence was never his forte, and the thought of actual contact with that vile individual made his skin crawl. Instead, he watched quietly with satisfaction as the scoundrel was manhandled down the sidewalk before being sent sprawling on his way.

Had he taken the trouble to watch the young man struggle painfully to his feet, he might have been quite surprised by the sad shake of the head as his eyes followed Scrooge's noble ascent up the marble staircase.

By the time Scrooge had reached the summit, he had already vanished into the encroaching darkness.

Security had cleared the lobby except for one lone cleaner. A Christmas tree adorned with twinkling lights and red bows enjoyed its transient celebrity status amid the opulent surroundings. The day after tomorrow, stripped of its baubles, it would be cast aside as trash, as though it had never been.

With a dismissive gesture, he waved Security away and crossed the deserted lobby alone. He paused to glance up at the tree.

"Enjoy, next week you'll be firewood," he informed the tree, to the consternation of the cleaner, who had been mopping the floor unnoticed by Scrooge.

The cleaner froze with her mouth open as she caught Scrooge's eye.

"Always talk to your plants, it helps make them more productive," he explained.

He pointed to the floor.

"I think you missed a bit."

She resumed her mopping with renewed vigour as she listened to the echo of his retreating footsteps.

This was his domain; he needed no protection, and the sound of his footfalls echoing off the marble floor reassured him. In truth, the encounter with the vagrant had unsettled him, as had the journey through the city's crowded streets. He had fallen asleep and experienced an unusually vivid dream, and that was all. Now he was nearly home.

His private lift was located at the end of a corridor accessible only through a hidden alcove. Very few people knew of its existence, which was the main reason why the sight of a young child standing beside the steel doors caused Scrooge to stop dead in his tracks.

The girl had her back to him. Long auburn hair cascaded over the back of her pink party dress. Scrooge guessed she was about nine or ten years old. Had one of the staff arranged a party without his knowledge? If so, there might be consequences.

"Children and business don't mix."

A familiar voice startled him, and he half turned to see who had taken the liberty of following him. Probably the same idiot who had brought the child into the building in the first place.

"What? Who's there?" he cried aloud.

Scrooge blinked, then rubbed his eyes as if trying to clear away a persistent fog that blurred his vision.

It made no difference; the corridor behind him was empty—not a soul in sight, only the startled cleaner who hurriedly grabbed her mop and bucket and darted away. He was clearly coming down with something. What he needed was a stiff whisky. The sooner he reached his suite, the better.

The child was still standing by the lift, now staring directly at Scrooge with sapphire blue eyes that reminded him of the feral Persian cat that had once slipped into the building unnoticed until he had come across one of the cleaners feeding it scraps. That had been the end of both the cat and the cleaner.

He opened his lips to demand an explanation for her presence, but his lips were dry, and his tongue clove to the roof of his mouth. As he watched, the elevator doors opened and she slipped inside. This was intolerable.

"Hey, kid, where do you think you're going?" he cried. "Wait!"

Scrooge sprinted towards the lift just in time to hold the doors open. He almost tumbled inside.

Perspiration trickled down his forehead, stinging his eyes. His breath came in short, heavy gasps. There would be a reckoning once he discovered who the girl's father was. Bringing a child to work and allowing her the freedom to run wild through his personal domain.

The lift was empty.

At first, he refused to believe the evidence of his own eyes. He closed them, counted to three, and reopened them, but the child was gone.

His collar felt unusually tight, constricting his breathing. He loosened his tie and slumped back against the cold, hard steel. His blurred image, reflected on the elevator's opposite side, also loosened his tie, but there was one difference.

Someone stood beside his reflection, looking up intently into his face—a child with auburn hair.

The reflection was hazy, as if he were seeing the scene through fogged glass, yet he believed her face expressed a profound sadness, and he was its source.

The doors swung open, and the familiar glow of his personal reception foyer beckoned him home.

"Good evening, sir. Is something the matter?"

Eva Perry, his personal secretary, stood outside the lift with a look of professional concern on her face, but Scrooge did not notice her expression. He was staring into the empty interior of the lift. Miss Perry moved forward and did the same.

"Have you lost something?" inquired Miss Perry.

"What?"

With difficulty, Scrooge tore his gaze away from the reflection of the child who now stood alone, her face still turned towards him.

"Would you mind taking a look inside, Miss Perry?"

She glanced at her employer as she stepped into the lift.

"Well?" he prompted. The urgency his voice conveyed could only mean that something of great significance was missing.

"What exactly am I looking for, sir?"

"You don't see her?"

"See whom? You were the only person in the lift, Mr Scrooge."

"A child, a little girl with auburn hair wandering around unaccompanied."

"No one is allowed on this level without your express permission and security clearance."

Was it possible he had been drinking this early? She knew his habits intimately; he was a man of strict routines and never took a drink before six at the earliest. Still, this was the festive season, and folk were more likely to drop their guard and overindulge at this time of year than at any other. No, this was Scrooge, after all—he was less likely to overindulge at Christmas than any man alive.

"I am fully aware I was the only person in the lift, Miss Perry. I just wondered if you had seen the child I described or some evidence that she had been inside the elevator."

"No, no children of any persuasion, sir."

He was lying, of that she was certain, but why?

Scrooge watched the elevator doors close. The child stood there watching him, trapped like a body floating beneath the surface of a shimmering metallic pool, until the doors shut completely, and she was gone forever.

A distant sound of music and children's laughter drifted up the corridor towards him. He stopped so suddenly that Miss Perry almost bumped into him.

"Do you hear that?" he asked.

"Hear what, Mr Scrooge?"

Miss Perry hoped he could not detect the note of concern in her voice.

"Has anyone authorised a children's party in my absence?" inquired Scrooge.

It was more an accusation than a question.

"Who would dare," replied Miss Perry coolly.

She smiled sweetly.

Scrooge looked at her suspiciously but said nothing.

"Can I get you a strong coffee?" she inquired innocently.

Scrooge disregarded the implication and headed towards the grand oaken doors that led to the boardroom.

"Make sure I am not disturbed for the next hour, Miss Perry."

"Someone is waiting to see you. He's been waiting quite a while."

Miss Perry nodded towards a stout man seated in one of the foyer chairs reserved for visitors. The man stood and tentatively raised his hand in a half-hearted greeting, but the stern expression on Scrooge's face caused him to sit back down.

"Then he'll have to wait a little longer," observed Scrooge.

Bravely ignoring the warning signs, Miss Perry persisted.

"But it is Christmas Eve, and he has been waiting over an hour."

"Your point being?" replied Scrooge.

Miss Perry and the individual exchanged glances. A faint smile briefly crossed his lips in acknowledgement of her failed attempt. Then he slumped back into the chair, adopting a decidedly dejected posture.

Without even acknowledging the individual's presence, Scrooge crossed the foyer and entered his private quarters. The solid mahogany doors closed behind him with a reassuringly heavy thud.

PART 2
CHRISTMAS EVE 6.00 P.M.

Tatters of desperate fog clung to the tower buildings, stubbornly resisting the freezing tug of the implacable wind. Like the hulks of submerged haunted wrecks emerging from some anonymous watery grave, the dark outline of the city took shape and grew.

Wisps of grey fog drifted mournfully past the windows of the monolith, which seemed almost to push and elbow its way above the mass of surrounding tower blocks, as though the very elements themselves shrank back from contact with the cold, indifferent stone.

Scrooge gazed out of the window.

Somewhere below, the river flowed blacker than the Styx through the city's dark heart into the eternal depths of the poisoned oceans. But Scrooge's eyes were fixed upon another river. The unceasing flow of humanity condemned to follow the course of existence to its inevitable conclusion as the river was compelled to flow into the embrace of the blind and restless sea.

Christmas held out hope that the journey was not in vain. That was one of the reasons he despised it. Christmas was for the weak, for sentimental fools who had never grasped that salvation in this world was something to be wrested forcefully from life's reluctant grip. Once the presents had been opened and the parties were over, what was left apart from hangovers and a bigger overdraft?

He smiled. He was above that now, had been for years. Just as detached and aloof as the gigantic reflection of himself superimposed on the vista upon which he cast such a scornful eye.

Scrooge blinked. Surely not!

It was his imagination. Sentimentality was infectious, but until now, he had considered himself immune to that particular disease. Yet what else could explain it? He rubbed his eyes.

Overwork had always been his way; he had often worked too hard. Perhaps he even needed a rest. There was no doubt about what he had seen. The reflection in the glass that once belonged to him was unquestionably that of Jake Marley, the very dead Jake Marley.

Slowly, he opened his eyes. There was nothing visible except his own reflection staring coldly back at him from above the city, like some eternally lost and disembodied soul.

Steady! This was very unlike him. He needed a drink, a stiff one. Scrooge abruptly turned away from the window and headed for the cocktail cabinet.

Usually, he never indulged except to toast a successful business deal or the demise, metaphorically or otherwise, of a competitor. After all, business is war. There are winners and losers. Scrooge has always been a winner, no matter what it takes. Sure, there are casualties; that's the nature of war, and Jake Marley was one of them.

That, however, had not been his fault. On that matter, his hands were clean and his conscience clear. Jake and he had been partners. True, Jake had always been a little soft, but what had happened had nothing to do with Ebenezer Clinton Scrooge III.

Then why was he troubled by an emotion so unfamiliar to him? Surely, this could not be guilt?

He poured himself a generous Scotch and sat down heavily in the chair at the head of the large, polished, rectangular boardroom table that, over the years, had become his personal domain.

The contents of the glass he downed in one go, catching his breath as the alcohol surged against the back of his throat. It had been a long time since he'd felt the need to down a drink with such urgency.

The last time was when the police had brought him the news about Jake. Jake had never gone for the deal in the first place. The subsequent board meeting was bitter and unyielding. Scrooge had persuaded the majority that the merger was in everyone's best interests, vital, in fact, to corporate survival.

It had been his finest hour. Jake had offered strong opposition, but as always, his argument was based on weakness, with the main thrust being that rather than a merger, the company was entering into a pact with Lucifer himself. You could almost smell the fire and brimstone. It was compelling stuff. Some of the Board had been spooked by Jake's vivid interpretation of the consequences.

Admittedly, there had been rumours, stories suggesting their potential partners were not entirely what they seemed. Jake had even gone as far as to suggest the company in question was merely a front for certain powerful and unscrupulous government agencies.

It was a perilous moment. Jake Marley was not a man who could easily claim the moral high ground in any argument, a fact Scrooge exploited mercilessly.

Scrooge reminded the Board that rejecting the merger on the grounds outlined by Jake would lead to litigation, serious litigation that the company could not afford. By the end of the meeting, the deal was almost signed and sealed, and the company was firmly under Scrooge's control. Jake proved a sore loser, muttering threats involving private investigators and the press.

Scrooge had invoked memories that played vividly before his eyes, even when he tried to shut them out.

The Boardroom, Manhattan 2000

He is no longer sitting at the table. He stands by the window, staring at the reflection of people enjoying themselves, as the party atmosphere infects everyone in the room with a kind of madness. Only he remains immune.

Someone is pushing their way through the revellers towards him. As the figure draws near, he recognises Jake Marley. Scrooge steels himself as Jake leans against the window and peers into his face.

"Come on, Ebenezer, loosen up and let your hair down, man."

Jake's words are more a challenge than an exhortation. Scrooge continues to gaze out the window.

"Never did like Christmas, did you, pal?"

Jake's voice is tinged with pity.

"Wanna hear something sure to put a smile on that sour puss?"

Suppressing his curiosity, Scrooge still ignores Jake.

"I'm leaving the company. Tendering my resignation."

This unexpected revelation provokes the response Jake had anticipated.

"You, retiring," exclaimed a sceptical Scrooge, "what will you do, write a book?" he added sarcastically.

Jake's reply stirs misgivings.

"That's exactly what I plan to do, Ebenezer," replied Jake, eyeing Scrooge intently. "Write a book, the book of revelations."

Scrooge's misgivings begin to take shape—unwelcome guests standing outside the threshold with evil tidings on their lips and vengeance in their hearts.

"If I were you, Jake, I'd stick to fiction," he advised, but his words carried a threat: "Autobiographies can be prejudicial to your health."

Jake looked at the man he had once called 'friend' as though seeing him clearly for the first time.

"'Prejudicial to my health'," he repeated the words slowly, "now you even sound like Michael Corleone."

Scrooge ignored the opportunity to lighten the tone of the exchange. Instead, his demeanour became even more intense.

"I'm serious, Jake," he said, almost pleading. "You have access to some very sensitive information."

It is now Jake who ignores Scrooge. He turns away and raises his glass to someone in the room.

"Hey, looking good tonight, Miss Perry!"

Eva Perry smiles and raises her glass in response.

"Why, thank you, Mr Marley," she shouted to be heard above the noise of people enjoying themselves.

Jake turned back to Scrooge, a gleam in his eye.

"You know Eva has a thing for you, don't you, Ebenezer?"

Scrooge looks confused.

"Evidently not," continued Jake.

"You're drunk," replied Scrooge defensively.

"I wish!"

Jacob held out his glass for Scrooge to inspect the contents.

"Tonic water! Truth is, my liver's shot; I haven't taken a drink in a year. The stuff's poison to me now."

He placed an unwelcome arm around Scrooge's shoulders.

"Come on, Ebenezer, let's go mingle with the minions."

Scrooge stepped back, avoiding any further contact.

"I've done my duty, I'm leaving."

There was a finality in Scrooge's voice that brooked no dissent.

"What's your problem?"

Jake was no longer smiling.

"It's not as if the lovely Valarie is still at home waiting for you."

"Thanks for the reminder," said Scrooge, his eyes hard and cold.

"Time to move on, Ebenezer, Valarie certainly has," observed Jake, twisting the knife with ease.

There was an awkward silence, eventually broken by Jake.

"Look, Eva's on her own over there."

Scrooge looked across the room to where Eva stood on the edge of the crowd. Was it his imagination, or did she keep glancing over in his direction? Scrooge dismissed it as merely a suggestion Jake had just mischievously planted in his head.

"I think I'll take a rain check," he declared.

"No kidding," commented Jake contemptuously, "see you around Ebenezer."

Jake began to walk away when Scrooge caught him by the arm.

"About that book," he said.

Jake smiled.

"Don't worry, Ebenezer, you get a whole chapter to yourself."

The smile disappeared as Jake wrenched his arm free and walked away.

Scrooge watched him cross the room. Eva smiled and raised her glass in his direction. Scrooge ignored her and turned back to the window.

The book was never written. Three weeks later, Jake's car, complete with Jake, was fished out of the river.

The coroner's verdict recorded 'death by misadventure', but the story circulated that high levels of alcohol had been found in Jake's blood—just another drunk driver who this time got his just desserts.

Only Scrooge and the rest of the Board knew that, although Jake had many vices, drink was no longer one of them. Excessive abuse in his younger days had devastated his liver. For the last year of his life, Jake was strictly teetotal, though that was where his temperance ended.

The Boardroom, Manhattan, February 2001

Scrooge listened to the news the two uniformed officers had brought. When they finished, he rose and shook each of them by the hand. He watched them leave, pausing at the door to let Eva pass, then they were gone.

Eva stared at the closed doors, then turned towards Scrooge, an expression of alarm shadowed her features.

"What did the police want?" she asked, a tremor in her voice.

Scrooge sat down heavily and leaned back in the chair to look at her.

"Not good news, I'm afraid, Eva," he said, adding to the sense of dread cramping her stomach.

"At least it's not the IRS," she replied, hoping humour might dispel the swelling waves of panic.

"Jake's dead."

It was a statement of fact, not an expression of grief—two words with the power to change lives forever.

"Mr Marley, he's dead?"

Eva shook her head.

"That's not possible. I was speaking to him on the phone last week."

"Some kind of accident," said Scrooge, filling out the detail.

"His car left the road and ended up in the river. He drowned."

Eva covered her mouth with her hand and sat down uninvited on one of the boardroom chairs.

"Poor Marcie, I have to call her," she exclaimed, getting back to her feet.

"Apparently, he was drunk," Scrooge announced.

The words stopped Eva in her tracks. She turned slowly to look at Scrooge.

"Drunk?" was her shocked response. "Didn't you tell them about his liver condition? Mr Marley has been on the wagon for over a year."

"Must have fallen off," replied Scrooge. "It's a blessing no one else was hurt."

"I guess," said Eva doubtfully. "That book he talked so much about will never get written now."

"That too," declared Scrooge, mistaking her meaning.

"Every dark cloud, Miss Perry."

Eva did not reply. She stared at Scrooge for a long time before turning on her heels.

"Wait!"

Eva stopped but did not turn round to face Scrooge.

"Arrange some flowers for the funeral, Miss Perry, spare no expense, it's tax-deductible."

Eva walked out without looking back. The door slammed shut behind her. Still, what was done was done. Jake was dead, and corporate life must go on.

The funeral had proved an embarrassment. Scrooge guessed it would when the family sent his flowers back, suggesting he might need some when his time came.

He had no choice but to attend, as his absence would only have fuelled some of the more wildly speculative and lurid rumours regarding his involvement in Jake's death.

Banquo probably felt more welcome at Macbeth's feast. Every time he glanced across, Jake's widow's eyes burned accusingly at him like hot coals through black smoke.

A face stared up at him from the polished surface of the table— a hard face. A face fashioned down the long years on the anvil of power by the hungry hammer of greed. Deep, humourless lines marked ruthless paths into the very essence of his being. Cold blue eyes stared from the depths of the table like the dead, empty eyes of a drowning man.

Scrooge flinched. Wherever possible, he avoided mirrors. Time had not been kind, or so he said. The truth was that Time had simply faithfully recorded the portrait of his life on the canvas of his face.

He was about to turn his head when the image in the table winked at him and grinned.

The solid oak chair spilt backwards as Scrooge leapt from the lips of a bottomless pit that seemed suddenly to be opening wide before him. His calves throbbed from the violent impact, but he could not avert his eyes, held as they were by a terrible fascination.

There could be no doubt, the reflection was that of Jake Marley. No mistaking the slightly lop-sided grin, the mischievous twinkle in those dark brown eyes and the compromising wink that always preceded some frivolous remark usually uttered at Scrooge's discomforted expense.

Nameless ice-cold insects crawled the length of his spine as the horror evolved and grew.

He gazed not upon the polished mahogany expanse of the table, but on the liquid surface of an oily pool in whose depths the body of Jake Marley slowly sank.

Jake Marley no longer winked, his eyes now black holes through which small fishes swam, his grin the skeletal grimace of a long-dead cadaver. Yet even as Scrooge watched, Jake's jawbone moved, as though trying to speak across the unbridgeable chasm that separates the living from the dead.

Words formed and took shape inside Scrooge's head, words that bubbled upwards from some dark watery subterranean place.

"Tonight, Ebenezer. Expect me tonight."

Other shapes drifted and floated around Jake Marley's receding form. Blue-black bloated bodies, arms extended in desperate and futile attempts to break the surface, reach out towards Scrooge, and drag him down to a dark and silent communion.

There were those he thought he recognised. Among them was a sacked employee who had taken his own life because he lacked the backbone to find another job. Quilp!

"Remember me, Mr Scrooge?" gurgled Quilp as its corrupted hands reached upwards, attempting to break the surface of the mahogany table.

"Remember us," echoed other corpses as they drifted towards the surface to swell the rotting ranks of the decomposing chorus.

Their eyes fixed on Scrooge as Jake's widow had done. Suddenly, they scattered like a shoal of frightened fish, because something was moving towards them out of the murky depths.

The rusted grill of a sunken limo came into view, looming larger and larger as it approached. Hunched over the wheel was a figure wearing a black fedora and trench coat.

Scrooge watched horrified as it drew near. Enough was enough! Clenching his fist, Scrooge smashed it down hard upon the table surface. It did not sink into unknown depths; instead, the shock of violent contact with an unresisting object reverberated painfully the length of his arm. His own face looked up at him, unforgiving.

The limo and its driver had returned to their watery grave.

"Must have been a bad batch of Scotch," he muttered.

"I'll sue the son of a bitch."

The prospect of suing someone partially restored Scrooge's good humour. Yet the boardroom table had become an alien and hostile object, a portal to dark worlds from which he shrank, forbidding his fevered imagination to step across the beckoning threshold. Could objects be alien and hostile? Surely that was the realm of fantasy and science fiction, and Scrooge was nothing if not pragmatic.

He needed to stretch his legs, move around, and get the blood circulating so it could deliver oxygen to his brain.

He found himself back at the window. Sweat beaded his brow. Perhaps he was sickening for something. The thought comforted Scrooge. If he was going to be sick, why not now? The festive season was a futile dissipation of Man's most precious commodity, Time. He despised the way it was squandered wantonly every year.

How many people really enjoyed Christmas anyhow? The obligatory family get-togethers, the gifts nobody wanted, the spoiled, ungrateful brats, quarrelsome and bored before the turkey had gone cold.

When the bank statement arrived in the post come January, the last Resolution evaporated before the chill winds of reality. Cynic he may be, but he always played the percentages, and cynics were rarely disappointed when the dice finally came to rest.

He watched the silver twinkling tail-lights slither like slugs' trails through the tangled undergrowth of buildings.

The windows of surrounding tower blocks were festooned with coloured lights and baubles. He guessed many would return to work, trying to forget the spectacles they made of themselves at the office party.

How Jake had enjoyed office parties. He always drank too much and flirted outrageously, but the staff seemed to love him for it. You can stab a man in the back on Tuesday, as long as you smile and buy him a drink on Monday, he won't suspect a thing.

Scrooge had grudgingly acknowledged Jake's capacity for duplicity. He had style, did Jake; you had to give him that. Look at him now, for instance.

Look at him now!

Scrooge blinked, but there he was, Jake Marley, hovering outside the window twenty-eight floors up, staring straight at Scrooge.

The fever was getting hold, or maybe the Scotch had been deliberately spiked with some hallucinogenic drug. Scrooge placed his hands on the windows for support and leaned forward.

He felt sick; was he going to faint? Scrooge despised weakness, but this was not weakness; this was either a deliberate and malevolent act of sabotage or an inane practical joke inspired by the lunacy that appeared to afflict the herd instinct at Christmas and the New Year. Regardless of the motivation, the consequence would be the same. Whoever was responsible was already dead in the water.

Why did he have to think of water?

An image of Jake sat at the seat of his submerged limousine, staring through hollow, sightless eyes as the eager fishes gathered filled his mind. He jerked his head upwards, and the image splintered and vanished.

His hands were still on the glass, but now they pressed against another pair of hands. Black-green mottled hands, the hands of Jake Marley. It was not the diseased hands of a long-dead man that forced a cry from Scrooge's lips, but the sight of a face pressed against the glass like a naughty schoolboy attempting to disrupt a class from which he had been expelled.

For a moment, they were eyeball to eyeball. Scrooge could even see his terror reflected in the glassy stare before he stumbled backwards.

The corpse of Jake Marley pressed against the window, and as it did so, the glass yielded before its weight, as though it were merely a thin film of plastic sheeting moulding itself against the grim contours of the rotting cadaver.

Instinctively, Scrooge shielded his eyes in anticipation of the imminent explosion of myriad shattered splinters of glass about to fly directly at him. Instead, the window yielded like the surface of a still pool closing silently above the form of Jake Marley as it tumbled onto the boardroom floor at the feet of Ebenezer Clinton Scrooge III.

Scrooge watched as logic wrestled with fear for control of his mortal coil. He only had to remain calm, and soon the effects of the drug would begin to diminish.

Jake Marley rose unsteadily, and as he did, droplets of water fell from his clothing, forming an icy pool at his feet. A fedora was pulled down low so that eyes gleamed from the shadows of its face, the lower portion of which was concealed behind a silk cravat, but there was no mistaking that this was the remains of his late business partner.

From deep within the silken folds, a familiar voice gurgled a greeting.

"Aren't you going to offer your old friend a drink? Sorry, I'm a bit late. You never could abide being kept waiting, could you, Ebenezer? Time was always too precious, your time in particular. Now, unlike you, Ebenezer, I have all the time in this world and beyond."

The creature doffed the fedora and bowed. Mercifully, long strands of matted wet hair covered its face.

"The late, very late Jake Marley at your service."

Scrooge was conscious of nails digging into the palms of his hand hard enough to draw blood.

"Maybe you figure I'm wet enough already."

It placed the fedora firmly back into place and stood upright as it spoke. The corpse laughed, and logic fled, leaving Scrooge at the mercy of a nameless terror. The dread sound was not of this world, nor did it evoke an image of heavenly choirs, but of darker, unforgiving entities that had not come to announce Good Will to All Men and Scrooge in particular, but tidings of an altogether different kind.

Scrooge squeezed his eyes shut tight and clasped his clammy hands hard over his ears. Like a child hiding from the Bogeyman, if he denied his brain sensory stimulation, his overheated imagination would cool, and the apparition return to the hidden depths of his subconscious from which it had risen unbidden.

The stench that assailed his nostrils was pure corruption, bottled and distilled in some charnel house in hell. Involuntarily, he opened his eyes and, gagging, covered his mouth with his hands.

"It's a long time since I brushed my teeth, Ebenezer."

Again, the horrid laughter echoes from another realm.

"You have no objections if I sit down?"

The gruesome phantom crossed to the head of the table and sat down in *the Chair*.

"Never thought I would achieve such an exalted position while you were still alive, Ebenezer. I think you had better join me, you look like you've seen a ghost."

A sound that might have once been described as a chuckle bubbled to the surface. Jake Marley pointed to the chair at the bottom end of the table directly opposite him. Scrooge was conscious of a distinct weakening of the knees, but he was damned if he was going to sit in that chair.

"Or maybe damned if you don't! There are many worse things than assuming the lowliest position in this life, Ebenezer. Much worse! Sit!"

Whether it was the effects of the spiked drink or the shock of realising that somehow the creature, rather the illusion, at the head of the table had read his thoughts, Scrooge complied with uncharacteristic meekness.

Of course, the thing could read his mind; it lived there. Whatever the next few moments brought, he had only to remind himself that its tenancy was temporary. Once restored to his normal mental state, the memory of Jake Marley would receive a permanent eviction order.

"Unless you see with your own eyes and touch with your own hands. You were ever the sceptic Ebenezer."

The creature leaned forward.

"You never listened to what I had to say. You never listened to anyone, except Ebenezer Clinton Scrooge III."

"That's not true, I always valued your opinion."

Careful, now he was beginning to argue with himself. He must hold tight to the fact that this thing was not real.

The creature leaned forward, elbows on the table, bringing the tips of its gloved fingers together as if it were examining Scrooge.

He imagined this was how a butterfly might feel before being impaled and displayed for eternity in a glass tomb. If there was one solace, it was that Jake's hands were now hidden in gloves. Wet, black, leather gloves that dripped a steady staccato beat on the surface of the table. Scrooge recognised the rhythm as that of his own pounding heart. The silence wrapped him like a weighted shroud. At last, the creature spoke.

"You valued my opinion, Ebenezer? How much?"

It paused, obviously awaiting a response.

There was no turning back now. He had crossed an invisible, intangible line, passing through a veil that separated reality from fantasy. Perhaps talking to oneself, even a self that assumed the form of a rotting corpse, was good therapy. Think positively; this need not be a negative experience; Scrooge hated waste of any kind. There was clearly an unresolved inner conflict that needed to be addressed. In the end, he would emerge refined and purged of contamination, the inevitable consequence of mingling with the common herd on a daily basis.

"How much?"

This last question was delivered with a vehemence that Jake Marley had never displayed in this life. Scrooge recoiled as the creature rose from its chair and pointed an accusing, corrupted finger at him.

"Um..."

Scrooge was rarely lost for words, but now they fled from his stuttering tongue like disturbed flies from a carcass.

"Thirty pieces of silver, Ebenezer, the eternal price of betrayal."

There was no longer anger in its voice but a sadness that reached out to Scrooge in a mournful embrace. Scrooge struggled free of its cloying grip. This was intolerable!

"Betrayal?"

He had intended to sound outraged, to plant his standard on the high pinnacle of moral ground, but was shaken by how his words stumbled feeble and defensive from his lips.

"There was never any betrayal, Jacob. It was business, pure and simple."

"Pure, pure, Ebenezer!"

Scrooge flinched before the creature's sarcasm.

"You truly believe business can clothe your sinful nature with respectability."

It shook its head solemnly.

"Ebenezer, you have walked this earth naked for many years."

It was not a comforting thought. Certainly not good for the corporate image. If it was true, why hadn't someone told him? While it had taken a child to wise up the emperor, he was afforded the privilege of an animated corpse who had apparently found religion since passing over to the Other Side. Steady, the phantom was obviously speaking metaphorically.

"Naked? I think not, Jacob, all my suits are genuine Armani, made to order and delivered personally."

His attempt at humour elicited no response. Humour had never been Scrooge's strength; he was always unable to distinguish it from sarcasm. The very tangible shade of Jacob Marley shook his head mournfully and, keeping his gaze fixed on his former partner, stood on 'the Chair' until he seemed to loom over Scrooge like some malevolent bird of prey, poised to strike.

Scrooge gazed up helplessly, resigned to his fate. This was one hell of a hallucination. Even as the thought slipped unbidden into his head, Jacob Marley's ravaged features reassembled themselves into what Scrooge assumed was a grin that somehow managed to radiate amusement and malevolence in equal measure.

"'Hell, Ebenezer. You think this is hell? Look within yourself, the fires are even now consuming your shrivelled soul."

This was the final straw. The only thing Scrooge felt consumed by at this moment was indignation. Driven by a sudden surge of righteous anger, he gripped the edge of the mahogany table and stared at the manifestation of his fevered imagination with steely resolve.

But the words of defiance died in a whimper on dry lips as he saw his twin self, small and lost, reflected in the Stygian darkness of those orbs. Plastic figures, trapped forever in a glass globe where no flakes of snow would ever fall to light the eternal darkness.

The being that had once been Jacob Marley stretched out a corrupted arm and pointed accusingly in his direction. Scrooge awaited the verdict without protest, resigned now to the possibility that he might actually be teetering precariously over the edge of madness.

"Ebenezer Clinton Scrooge III, tonight you are condemned to confront your worst nightmare. Not once, not twice, but three times before the clock strikes midnight."

Despite the rising panic, Scrooge could not suppress a growing irritation at the way Jake was beginning to sound more and more like an ageing thespian, hamming up his final appearance before ignominy consumed him forever.

Jake paused.

Scrooge waited.

"Tonight," Jake continued, and Scrooge was almost persuaded he could detect a tone of amusement in the measured pronouncement of doom, "you will receive three invitations. "

What horrors awaited him? Before his mind's eye lurid visions of humiliation, pain and terror emerged like ephemeral shapes out of some primordial mist, only to fragment and vanish as others more awful in their intensity took substance in their place.

Scrooge, mute with apprehension, awaited judgment. But none came. Instead, the creature slowly removed the silk cravat from the lower portion of his countenance.

"Because I just know how you love parties, Ebenezer."

As soon as the last words were spoken, the Jake-Thing slipped the cravat off completely and hurled it at the trembling Scrooge. It fluttered unnoticed to the floor, but what captured Scrooge's full attention was the way Jake's jaw dropped open, striking the mahogany surface of the boardroom table several feet below with a sickening thud. This was accompanied by an unearthly howling that could have been laughter, but whose source was something less human.

Scrooge screamed as he felt his fingers being forcibly prised away by some external and malevolent force from his tenuous grip on reality. Below, a yawning void beckoned. But it was not Scrooge who plunged headlong into the darkness, for before he could avert his terrified eyes, he witnessed the final confirmation of his temporary state of madness.

Jacob Marley launched himself from the chair, as though he were diving into the swimming pool he once loved to cavort in with his various lady friends back in his old Malibu mansion.

The polished surface yielded before him, and closed above him, and Jacob Marley was gone.

Gone? He was never really here!

A sudden hammering on the boardroom door reverberated through Scrooge's tense frame like an electric current. No, it was not possible. Slowly, the door swung open. Only the solid mass of mahogany kept him from falling.

"Are you all right, sir?"

Suppressing an almost irresistible desire to whoop with relief, Scrooge stoically held his emotions in check and merely nodded, unable to trust himself to speak. Thank God, normality had returned.

"You look rather pale."

Miss Perry, his personal secretary, did not usually inquire about his health, so he guessed tonight's 'experience' had left a visible impression.

"Only there's someone who'd like to speak with you if it's convenient."

Mistaking her employer's silence as a sign of displeasure, she added with characteristic charity.

"He's been waiting a long time, and it is Christmas Eve."

"How long has he been waiting?"

His eyelid began to twitch. That hadn't happened since 8th Grade. When would this nightmare end?

"He should have left about an hour ago, sir."

"An hour," exclaimed Scrooge, "it seemed more like a lifetime."

"Excuse me?"

Eva's eyes narrowed as she studied Scrooge carefully.

"Anyway, what with it being Christmas Eve and the traffic and everything... are you sure you don't want a glass of water or something? You look like you've seen a..."

"Thank you, no!"

The vehemence in his voice even startled Scrooge. Miss Perry took a step backwards onto safer ground.

"Just show him in. Then you can go, Miss Perry."

"Very well, sir, and Merry Christmas."

She waited, evidently expecting a response.

"What? Yes, you also, Miss Perry."

Scrooge watched her back away, her eyes betraying mingled alarm and relief. Muffled voices echoed outside, followed by a tentative rap on the door.

"Come!"

Scrooge hoped that the anxiety he felt rising like floodwaters had not yet reached his voice. The door opened slightly, and an overweight, middle-aged, nondescript individual squeezed into the boardroom, wearing an ingratiating smile that Scrooge found instantly offensive.

"Well?"

Scrooge was relieved to recognise the man as an employee working in Accounts somewhere. Incredibly, he even thought he remembered the person's name, Bobby Scratchitt, or something very similar.

Hadn't his brother died on 9/11? He vaguely remembered a memo from Miss Perry about a sympathy card. Given the circumstances, it was the politically correct thing to do, so he had given her permission to go ahead on his behalf. He might even have signed it.

The man was shifting uneasily from foot to foot. It wasn't helping Scrooge's frayed nerves, already stretched to breaking point.

"Spit it out, man, I don't have all night!"

"No Ebenezer Scrooge, you have Eternity."

Did Scratchitt, if it truly was Scratchitt, really say those words, or was it a dislodged fragment of his hallucinogenic ordeal? Maybe Scratchitt was the culprit. Nobody could possibly be as inoffensive as he looked.

He took a tentative step towards his employee, half expecting the rancid form of Jake Marley to burst through the meek veneer of Scratchitt like some hostile alien entity, leaving the man's discarded skin in a crumpled heap on the floor.

Intimidated by his employer's aggressive manoeuvre, Bob Cratchitt stepped back, but not before Scrooge lurched forward, thrusting a bony finger into his chest. This was not going according to plan. He seemed to have antagonised his boss even before opening his mouth.

Yet the very act of physical contact appeared to calm Scrooge's more aggressive tendencies. An expression of what could only be described as relief flooded his features. Had he been drinking? Maybe that's why he kept himself locked away in his suite like some latter-day Howard Hughes.

"Well, Scratchitt?"

For a brief moment, Bob Cratchitt thought he glimpsed a flicker of a smile crossing those thin lips. Then it vanished, like a pale winter sun hidden behind a darkening storm cloud.

"Scratch what, Mr Scrooge, sir?"

He was beginning to feel distinctly uneasy about Scrooge's strange behaviour, and this last request had done nothing to alleviate his mounting apprehension. Mentally, he started to calculate the distance to the door. If it came to a footrace, he wasn't in the best of shape, and the thought of having to turn his back on a violent alcoholic projected vivid images of wanton violence on the blank screen of his imagination, like trailers for a Tarantino movie.

Scrooge rubbed his eyes. A staccato throbbing at his temples warned him of an impending headache. What was the fool talking about?

"Just state your business, Scratchitt, " he was about to add, "I have a home to go to."

But that would have been a lie. Not that he subscribed to the peculiar moral reservations many weaker individuals held regarding the 'truth', as they perceived it.

A lie was a useful tool, a formidable weapon in the hands of skilled and ruthless people. It was just that this specific lie discomforted him. Truth was, it caused him pain, but he could not admit to such vulnerability, especially to himself.

"Cratchitt, sir, Bob Cratchitt. Not Scratchitt."

An immense wave of relief washed over Bob Cratchitt. Scrooge had not been requesting any perverse physical contact; he'd just mispronounced his name. Now they would both laugh at the misunderstanding, and the tension would ease. He could make his request in a more conducive atmosphere. He might even leave on first-name terms.

"Whatever! Is that it? We've got your name wrong on the payroll?"

Hope shrivelled at Scrooge's feet, a cowed dog no longer able to please its master. Bob Cratchitt swallowed hard. It would be easy to back down. Too easy. That was something Bob Cratchitt had been practising all his miserable, failed life. But this was not about him.

"Sir, my boy Timmy, he's real sick."

He'd promised himself he would not get emotional, but an image of Timmy's wasted little body threatened to overwhelm his defences, and he swallowed hard.

Scrooge studied Cratchitt as he would the minute details of some long and complex business contract, but the subtle nuances of human behaviour remained a closed book to him, as they always had.

Interpreting Bob Cratchitt's emotional turmoil as an indication that he had concluded what he had come to say, Scrooge gestured dismissively that the audience was over.

"Very well, Scratchitt, I'll get Payroll to amend your details, and I'm sorry to hear about your boy. Now shut the door behind you on your way out."

The guy had waited over an hour just because someone had misspelt his name in Payroll, really! Why was he still standing there? He glowered at Cratchitt, but the man seemed to be in some kind of catatonic trance.

Just as he decided it would be prudent to summon security, the man opened his mouth and spoke. The words seemed forced from Cratchitt's lips, as if reluctant to expose themselves to the withering intensity of Scrooge's scrutiny.

"It's not about my name. I need more time off. An extension of my Christmas holiday. I don't want to be paid or anything."

This evening was getting weirder and weirder. Scrooge was momentarily nonplussed. Had he heard correctly? Was the man really asking for a longer holiday? But before he could respond, Scratchitt spoke again, and this time the effort seemed to drain him of all his vitality.

"This will probably be Timmy's last Christmas. I want to spend more time with him while I can."

So that was his game. Playing the old sympathy card. Did the guy know who he was dealing with?

"Very well, Scratchitt. Take an extra week."

Wait for it, Scrooge smiled inwardly, here comes the sting in the tail.

"But you lose your two weeks' vacation in the summer. You know full well the New Year is our busiest time."

Masterstroke! Once word got passed around that Scratchitt had lost a week instead of gaining one, no one else was likely to repeat an exercise so inevitably doomed to failure.

Strange, why was Scratchitt smiling? Sure, it was a weak smile, like a pale winter sun, but a smile nonetheless.

"Thank you, Sir," he replied, looking genuinely grateful.

This guy could act.

"I won't be needing another vacation this year."

What had he missed?

Whatever angle Scratchitt was working, Scrooge hadn't figured it out yet. But he would, and when he did, Scratchitt wouldn't know what hit him. He'd have this guy watched closely from now on in. It was just a matter of time before he slipped up.

"And you have plenty of Time, don't you, Ebenezer?"

That voice again! It couldn't possibly be Scratchitt because he was already halfway across the boardroom. It was amazing someone of his size could move that fast.

"Wait a minute, Scratchitt."

Scratchitt froze. His hand gripped the brass door handle so tightly that Scrooge could see the fleshy knuckles turn white. Scrooge could hear his heavy breathing from across the room.

"Did you just say something?"

Bob Cratchitt froze, his brain simply refusing to respond. What did the man want from him? Surely, he wasn't going to change his mind. Or perhaps he hadn't; maybe he had never intended to give him the extra week in the first place. Even worse, it was a perverse test he must pass before he could escape with the precious gift of seven days that would never come again but would stay with him and Ellen forever.

Why couldn't he think? The clock was ticking so loudly that he couldn't concentrate. Soon, it would be Christmas Day. Of course! Christmas! A rabbit set free from a snare could not have felt more relief. He turned towards Scrooge, his face beaming.

"Merry Christmas, sir, Merry Christmas and a Happy New Year!"

The man was obviously a few bottles short of a full cellar. Merry Christmas! His kid was sick, he'd just lost a week's holiday, and the imbecile stood there grinning as if auditioning for the part of Quasimodo. Bells were definitely ringing in this guy's head. H.R. had probably employed him to keep the Politically Correct Lobby sweet. What a sad world we live in!

"Just get out and shut the door behind you, Scratchitt."

The smile died prematurely on Cratchitt's lips. Wordlessly, he complied meekly with his employers' command.

The door creaked as it shut tight like a coffin lid in an ancient Gothic vault. A coffin lid! Get a grip. The evening's events were forcing Scrooge to face an uncomfortable reality. He had been working too hard, and this was obviously his body's way of forcing him to confront the situation. His nerves were a little frayed, that's all.

He sat down heavily on one of the padded walnut chairs, studiously avoiding the one that appeared to have a damp patch spreading across its surface like a dark stain.

A drink! Another drink! Two in one night, this was becoming a habit. If he wasn't careful, he'd end up like Valarie. He pushed the thought away as he would an unwelcome guest. He would not go there. Valarie was the past, the distant past, and that is where she would stay. His eyes turned towards the window.

Outside an electric firmament of lights lit the darkness, where an endless supply of Valarie's was readily available to a man of Scrooge's wealth and power, without the suffocating downside of attachment and commitment.

Preoccupied by his thoughts, Scrooge could not recall physically crossing the boardroom floor to the drinks cabinet. He stood for a moment, blinking in disbelief. There was the bottle of

Scotch he had opened, and propped against it was a white envelope. It had not been there before, or had it?

"What's this, a cheap card from Scratchitt?"

He eyed the envelope suspiciously, debating whether to summon Miss Perry and ask her to open it; in these precarious times, one could not be too careful. The envelope bore his name, not 'Ebenezer' or 'Mr. Scrooge' or even 'Clinton', a name it was universally understood he detested, but simply 'Benny'.

No one had called him that in years. It was a name that only one other person knew, because she had bestowed it affectionately upon him. It could only be one other, his sister Leah. "

Leah!" he gasped.

He picked up the letter as though it were a fragile and precious object. For a long, still moment, he stared in disbelief. The hand holding the letter dropped to his side, and he leaned against the bar for support and gazed into a distant, painful past.

Scrooge's House in the Suburbs, Christmas 1990

Scrooge stood on the porch watching a woman with auburn hair hurry down the driveway carrying a small suitcase. At the end of the driveway, his sister Leah is standing alongside a yellow cab. Scrooge steps off the porch.

"Valarie, wait! We can work this out."

Valarie ignored his plea, and his words were snatched away on the chill winter wind. She and Leah embraced as the cab driver placed Valarie's suitcase in the trunk. Leah had obviously spared no expense. The cabbie wore a peak cap associated with firms at the upper end of the market, and his shades were surely only for show.

He opened the door for Valarie, and Scrooge suddenly realised this was for real. Abandoning his pride, he ran headlong down the drive.

"Valarie, please!"

The cabbie closed the door with a thud, and Valarie sat as still as stone on the back seat, staring straight ahead. Scrooge attempted to look through the window, but Leah stepped in his way.

"She needs space, Benny," she said softly, "she's hurting right now. She lost her baby, remember."

"Our baby," protested Scrooge.

Leah was about to speak, but appeared to think better of it.

An awkward silence settled between them.

Leah lowered her head, in a conscious effort to compose herself before speaking.

"Don't you realise what day it is, Benny?" she asked, searching his face.

"Sure," he replied bitterly, "what do you want me to say, Leah, 'Merry Christmas'?"

Sadness clouded Leah's eyes.

"It's Christmas Eve, Benny, the baby was due today."

She waited for a response. None came.

"She's going to stay with me for a little while, that's all."

"You taking her side against me? That it, Leah?"

Outrage, anger, and sadness laced his words like a poisonous, potent cocktail.

"I'm not taking anyone's side, Benny; I'm just being a friend."

Leah's words were heavy with sorrow.

"Blood, Leah," persisted a desperate Scrooge, "blood is thicker than water. You came for me, remember? When nobody cared, you came. I told you everything, Leah, all those dark, dirty secrets."

Tears coursed down Scrooge's cheeks. Leah placed a comforting hand on his arm.

"I wish I'd come for you sooner, Benny," she said, failing to hold back the flow of her own tears. "I'll always be here for you, baby."

Leah moved forward to embrace her brother, but he pulled away, hurt in his eyes.

"Then why are you betraying me?"

It is the cry of a child lost in the dark.

Leah is stricken with remorse. All she can do is shake her head as the tears blind her eyes.

"You do this and you're dead to me, Leah," said Scrooge, and she knew it was not an empty threat. "Do you understand?"

"Dead?"

Leah repeated the word slowly as though it were bitter on her tongue.

"What about Stephen? Is he dead to you, too? He worships you, Benny."

Scrooge turned away and walked back towards the house without answering.

"Benny!" cried Leah.

"Sorry, lady, but I have another pick up waiting," said the cabbie as he opened the passenger door. "Are we good to go?"

Leah nodded and climbed into the cab alongside Valarie. The driver shut the door behind her. Valarie did not look back.

From the porch, Scrooge watched the cab drive off until it disappeared into the distance. He turned away and entered the house, slamming the door behind him, sending the Christmas wreath crashing to the floor.

This was a place he did not want to go. Even after all these years, the memories were still too raw and painful. It was Leah who had sought him out through half the orphanages in the State. It was to her he had revealed his shameful secret, and she who had begun the healing process.

When Valarie left him, it was to Leah she had turned, and Leah had betrayed him. She took Valarie in, took her part against him, and, in so doing, severed the bond between them. Leah's act was not merely a betrayal; it was something much more: a judgment.

Surely, she of all people understood the reason why the course he had taken was the best for everyone, including Valarie.

His fingers were drawn to the black ink on the white parchment. Slowly, they traced the neatly written letters in silent rebellion to their master's command. Helpless as a child confronted with a brightly wrapped gift, he tore open the envelope and let it flutter like a dead leaf to the floor.

As he unfolded the cheap writing paper, he noticed his hands were trembling. This was ridiculous. Even Jacob's foul spectre had not unnerved him as much as this ragged piece of paper, but Jacob's words had not the power to wound as did those he now held in his hands.

For a moment, he was tempted to crumple the letter into a ball and cast it aside, as he had done metaphorically many times before. Miss Perry had been well schooled and instructed on what mail was never to reach his personal in-tray. Which raised another question: how had it gotten past Eva in the first place? Christmas was no excuse for a lack of vigilance. That could wait.

He forced his eyes towards the first line, and the salutation hooked him as surely as a skilled fisherman snares a trout.

"Dearest Benny, it has been a long time since I heard from you. Too long. Perhaps one day you can find time to reply to one of my letters. So much has happened. But I want you to know that Valarie is well, and the baby is doing just fine. A little boy like her with a full head of auburn hair. She has put the past behind her and wishes you well. . ."

Leah would never know the pain her words inflicted. Had she done so, she would never have written them. The implication was clear: Valarie had chosen to conceal the real reason behind her 'miscarriage'.

An uncomfortable sensation enveloped him. He could not name it, for Guilt had always been excluded from his presence by Expedience and Reason. Yet it was the revelation that Valarie now had a child of her own that made him physically recoil, as if struck a blow that rendered him defenceless.

". . . Not all my news is as cheerful. Stephen left three weeks ago, and I haven't heard from him. It's been four months since he came home. He is so changed, Benny. It's not the physical changes the blast inflicted on him, although God knows they are bad enough, it's as if the old Stephen died and a stranger came back in his body. . ."

Stephen? He vaguely remembered a blonde-haired child with twinkling eyes that made you feel you were looking at his mother. Stephen had enlisted. Obviously, he shared his mother's idealistic tendencies. Always wanting to change the world, but the world was a hard place to change. He knew that, and so now, did Stephen.

"Stephen joined the Marines," Scrooge reflected.

Helmut Province, Afghanistan, 18 Months Earlier

He could hear men shouting, their voices echoed hollowly, drifting up from some distant tunnel. Someone had screamed, but it was quiet now. Had it been him?

His eyes began to clear. Shapes were moving towards him through a swirling dark cloud.

A deafening roar drowned every sound, and he realised a helicopter was landing close by. His mind began to focus again, and he recalled the explosion before the darkness enveloped him.

He looked down at where his arm should have been, and this time, when he screamed, it was not just the pain.

"Hold tight, soldier, we're taking you home."

A medic was kneeling over him.

He tried to reply, but the merciful darkness consumed him once more.

Scrooge read it again and felt a tightening in his gut.

". . . He is so changed, Benny. It's not the physical changes the blast inflicted on him, although God knows they are bad enough, it's as if the old Stephen died and a stranger came back in his body. . ."

"Why the hell didn't he come to me? I'd have helped set him up."

Leah's Home, 1988

Leah and her six-year-old son, Stephen, are sitting together on a sofa reading a book when the door opens, and Scrooge enters. Stephen leaps off the sofa and runs towards him, flinging his arms around Scrooge's waist.

"This is a surprise," declares an excited Leah, "must be something very important to tear you away from your precious work."

Scrooge lifted a delighted Stephen onto his shoulders.

"She already told you, didn't she?"

Scrooge studied his sister carefully. Leah did not attempt to deny it.

"Of course, she did," Leah was practically bursting, "do you think a girl could keep a secret like that from her best friend? I'm so happy for both of you, Benny."

Leah stood and embraced her brother.

"You may be having a new little cousin before long, Stephen," she said with a twinkle in her eye.

Scrooge backed away slightly.

"Whoa there, Leah," he protested, "babies are going to have to wait. Children and business don't mix."

Leah's smile faded as Scrooge lifted Stephen to the ground and took him by the hand.

"Come on, soldier, let's go play outside."

Leah watched them go.

". . . He began to drink heavily, and I think he was taking drugs. I tried to talk to him, but he got so angry. He frightened me sometimes, Benny. Once, when we argued, he threatened to leave, saying he was going to find some of his ex-army buddies living rough in New York City. Now he's gone. I know it's a long shot, but I thought he might come looking for you if he got desperate. . .

"I would have sent him on his way, sir, but he says he knows you."

Grainger's words echoed in his head like distant thunder. The vagrant's ruined face filled Scrooge's vision. The disfigured features, the missing limb, the bright blue eyes that for a moment held his own. He sees its lips move, but it is as if everything has slowed down. Even the vagrant's voice is distorted. Could it be possible?

Well, it was too late now, whatever. Maybe it was for the best. Self-pity was a disease, and now the source of the infection had been removed from his sister's presence.

". . . You probably won't even read this letter, Benny. Have you ever read any of the ones I've sent you? It's just I'm pretty desperate right now, and it is Christmas, you know, when light

What she wanted was something he could not give. . . hope.

To offer hope when there was none was the worst form of abuse. Once, hope had been his only companion, and each new day, they waited expectantly for a loving family to deliver him from the endless nightmare of the orphanage.

Hope was deceitful and cruel, a false friend, and eventually he shut it out. He crumpled the letter in his hands and tossed it into the bin. It was too late now, too many bridges had been burnt, and the rivers were too deep and wide. But it was as if the very act drained him of his strength. He grasped the bottle of Scotch and sat down heavily on the nearest chair.

Scrooge awoke to find the bottle of Scotch half empty. By way of compensation, something with large boots had taken up residence inside his head.

Someone was hammering on the door. He struggled to his feet, levering himself up with one hand pressed down on the hard bed.

Hard bed! He rubbed his eyes, then opened them wide.

He must still be asleep. There could be no other explanation.

A little boy in grey, shabby shorts stared back at him from the mirror on the tiny dressing table. Behind him, the faded rose-patterned wallpaper he detested with a passion formed a gaudy background to his small frame.

The door opened. Miss Stryker stood looking at him as though she had just discovered a stain on her starched white blouse.

"Dinner is in ten minutes. Be there, or the dog gets it. If I had my way, he already would have."

Scrooge felt himself stare back defiantly through the child's eyes.

All those years had passed, and she was long since cold in her grave, but still her memory invoked a bitterness he could taste fresh on his tongue.

"You're a wicked boy, Ebenezer. Those terrible lies you told about Mr Izzard."

The boy remained silent, staring down at the floor. Scrooge yearned to scream his denial at her, to affirm the truth she denied, but he was merely a guest. Although physically a helpless spectator, his emotions were one with the child he had left so far behind.

"You will be pleased to know that all charges have been dropped. Mr Izzard will be back with us in the New Year. We should all be thankful the damage you inflicted was not more permanent."

In response to her words, his stomach cramped violently, and he almost gagged as he felt the acid sting of bile at the back of his throat.

How could he have forgotten what it felt like? Something wet struck his hand, and he realised they were tears. His tears.

"Were you thinking of going somewhere, Ebenezer?"

She inclined her head in the direction of his feet, and for the first time, he noticed the small battered brown suitcase lying by his bed.

"You'll need a coat."

She plucked his jacket from the chair that stood by the dressing table and tossed it carelessly onto the bed.

"It's started snowing."

He looked out the window. Fresh glistening flakes of snow drifted past the grey tenement blocks, only to be trodden underfoot by the restless flow of humanity that daily passed him by. Did he bury his head in his hands, or was it the child? Both wept silent tears that flowed from a wellspring deeper than despair.

"Merry Christmas, Ebenezer."

The door slammed shut. It seemed an eternity he remained sitting on the bed, his head buried in his hands.

He was reminded of the story of Ulysses, who ordered himself bound to the mast so he could hear the cries of the Harpies that drove men to their doom. Whatever Power was at work, it had bound him with invisible bonds to the body and mind of this helpless child.

His body shook as the boy sobbed himself to sleep, and the blessed relief of oblivion.

Scrooge awoke suddenly.

Someone was outside the door again, knocking gently. He swung his feet off the bed and half-stumbled into a large holdall by the side of the bed.

What had become of the battered old suitcase? Perhaps they had packed all his belongings while he slept and were now intending to throw him out. Where would he go?

The knocking persisted, and he heard a soft, gentle voice.

He regained his balance by gripping the dressing table, and in that moment gazed into the mirror. The child was gone. Staring back at him suspiciously was the thin, gaunt face of a young man who reminded Scrooge of an animal that had been badly treated, and now regarded the world and everything in it with a deep distrust.

"Benny, Benny, it's me, Leah. Please open the door."

"Come in. It's never locked."

He heard himself speak, yet it was not his voice, just an echo from the distant past.

"Benny, what's wrong? You haven't changed your mind?"

With difficulty, he turned away from the young man in the mirror, knowing he would never see his face again.

"No, of course not. I just thought you might not come."

He watched the tears well in her eyes and noticed how the sunshine reddened her hair like a wounded halo. She rushed forward and embraced him. He did not resist, but he could not respond. The smell of her perfume was still precious to him; it spoke of the warmth he had never known until then.

"Do you think I'd let you go after finding you at last, Benny?"

She took him by the hand and led him out of the room, closing the door quietly on his lost childhood. He paused on the landing.

"My things," he said.

Leah gripped his hand tightly.

"Is there anything you really want?" she asked.

He shook his head.

"Tomorrow, we'll go shopping."

She led him down the stairs. Even then, he could not believe his deliverance was at hand. Izzard or Stryker would at any moment appear like vengeful angels and bar the way, but they never did. As they walked down the grey stone steps towards the waiting limousine, Leah slipped her arm inside his.

"Come on, Benny, there's a whole new life waiting for you," she promised her brother as he hesitated on the top of the steps, as though the house was reluctant to let him go.

Scrooge did not look back. They stepped onto the sidewalk, and Doug, Leah's adopted father, moved forward and shook his hand warmly.

"Pleased to meet you at last, Ebenezer. Leah hasn't stopped talking about you."

Doug ushered Scrooge towards the limo.

"Come on, Ebenezer, let's take you home."

Leah climbed into the back of the limo and patted the seat beside her. Scrooge hesitated and turned to look up at the window of the only 'home' he has ever known.

A young child looks down at him longingly.

"What's the matter, son?" said Doug, concern in his voice.

It is the first time he can remember anyone calling him 'son'.

"I just thought," he began, glancing back up at the window, but the child was no longer there.

"It doesn't matter," he said and climbed into the car.

He sank into the plush upholstery and closed his eyes as the door slammed shut, and the car moved away down the darkening street. From the window, the shadow of the child he once had been watched helplessly, as the young man he had become passed out of view without looking back.

Something had been 'lost' that even Leah could not find. Although they were happy years spent with Leah's adoptive father, they were never enough to fill the void that had opened inside him.

Doug had treated him as though he were his own, but there are bonds that can only be forged early in life when the spirit is pliable and open and uncontaminated by the world.

Still, there were times he remembered that were good when happiness seemed almost within his grasp. The motion of the car and Leah's soothing presence lulled him to sleep.

He opened his eyes and blinked, dazzled by the lights.

They were no longer in the limo. Doug stood next to him in a room filled with people, laughter, and conversation. In the background, Christmas music was playing. He was staring at a Christmas tree festooned with coloured lights and bright baubles.

By the tree, two attractive women were deep in conversation. Every so often, they would glance over in his direction and smile.

"Get over there, man, before someone else beats you to it. Truth is, if I were thirty years younger."

Doug was standing over him, grinning like a Cheshire cat, the way he always did when he'd drunk a little too much.

"Doug? It can't be you?"

"What are you mumbling about now, boy?"

"Nothing, I was thinking aloud, is all."

"That's your trouble, Ebenezer, you think too much. Just get over there and speak to the girl."

"What girl?"

"What girl? You crack me up, Ebenezer. The one with auburn hair in the red silk dress, the girl you and all the other young bucks in the room have been drooling over all night."

"Oh, that girl."

"Now's your chance while she's talking to Leah."

"Maybe it's a private conversation, you know, girl talk."

Scrooge knew he was the subject of their conversation. Leah had told him later. She had been so happy for him. The girl with auburn hair glanced over at Scrooge before directing her question at Leah.

"So, what's the story, Lea?"

"Story?" replied Leah, feigning innocence.

Her friend was not fooled.

"You were adopted, right? So where did you find your brother?"

Leah hesitated a moment before answering.

"In a state institution, an orphanage."

Her friend peeked across at Scrooge over her glass.

"Poor guy, I've heard those places can be pretty rank."

"He never talks about it," said Leah.

Valarie eyed Leah quizzically. Her response had been a little too quick, like it always was when she was lying.

"It's been great for Stephen having a man around, seeing how his own father doesn't want to know," she replied, attempting to move the conversation away from the orphanage.

Her friend smiled that slow, bewitching smile of hers.

"Sounds like he could do with some TLC himself," she observed. Why don't you call him over?"

Leah looked distinctly uncomfortable.

"I told you, Val, he's vulnerable right now."

Valarie appeared to find this amusing.

"You his sister or his mother? Don't worry, Lea, I'll be a pussy cat."

Leah sighed. She is never able to resist Val anything. She looks over to where Doug and her brother are standing.

"She's been glancing over at you all evening, Ebenezer", observed Doug. "Anyway, you've got no choice now, Leah is calling you."

Leah was indeed gesturing for Scrooge to join them.

"Right," he said with a marked lack of enthusiasm.

"Good luck, son."

Doug, it couldn't be.

Doug died from a massive stroke a long time ago. Memories surfaced their way unbidden to his captive consciousness, and he knew with dread certainty where he was. Imprisoned in the body of his former self, he found himself moving forward.

He knew instinctively where he was going, just as surely as the doomed moth senses the heat of the flame but is powerless to resist.

He wanted to turn and run, but felt the unfamiliar constriction of his facial muscles instead as they formed a spontaneous smile. If only he could force his eyes shut. Surely this nightmare must end soon.

She was standing with her back to him, wearing the red silk dress that revealed her milk white skin, over which auburn hair glistened like fresh leaves in the fall. Leah saw him and motioned for him to join them.

It was only then that Valarie turned towards him and smiled, a smile that still haunted him down a lifetime of sleepless nights.

He had almost forgotten just how breathtakingly beautiful she was. At that moment, he would have given anything for the power to turn and walk away.

"Benny, this is my very best friend, Valarie. She's been dying to meet you."

Valarie blushed in response but did not attempt to deny it. They gazed at each other without speaking—two lovers clutching tickets for a first-class berth on the Titanic.

Why did they have to meet then? The timing was all wrong. Doug had managed to secure him a position in the Company, and he was determined to be a success. Relationships were a diversion; they could wait until he was financially secure and invulnerable.

He would never be that little boy again, alone and dreading the dark.

"Hello, Valarie."

"Please, my friends, call me Val."

"Will you excuse me a moment? I think Dad wants me."

Leah diplomatically excused herself.

"Well, this is cosy."

"Yes, it is."

"What should I call you?"

"Me? Uh, Eb. . . Benny, call me Benny."

She was smiling up at him. His collar felt unusually tight. The room began to spin, and instinctively, he shut his eyes.

Delmonico's, New York City, May 1990

"Benny, are you alright? Did you hear what I said?"

He was no longer standing. Had he fainted and made a fool of himself?

Valarie was leaning forward across the table, holding his hand, a look of concern on her face.

She was no longer wearing the red silk, but a plain Camille crochet grey dress that showed off her great legs. It was the last time she had ever worn it.

Delmonico's was full, but her soft tone cut through the din like an archangels' trumpet. He saw the fear and uncertainty in her eyes as she awaited his response.

"Yes, I heard." Scrooge withdrew his hand.

She flinched, then lowered her head submissively, preparing herself for the inevitable blow to fall.

"It's just not the right time for us. Perhaps in a few years, when I've established myself. Babies and business don't mix."

How hollow his words sounded, even then.

"That's the thing with babies, Benny, they have their own timetables. What do you suggest? Should I send it back?"

His silence uttered the words he did not dare to speak.

"Oh no, Benny, not that. You can't ask me to do that?"

She leaned back in her chair, a wounded animal ready to take flight.

"It's for the best, Baby, believe me. It's a hard world out there, and when we bring a child into it, I want to be sure it's going to have the best."

He leaned forward to cover her hand, but this time she pulled away and stood so forcefully that her chair tumbled backwards onto the floor, attracting some attention from the adjacent tables. ,

"Valarie, wait!"

But she had taken flight.

He left money on the table and followed her out into the night. There was a chill in the air, and she had gone without her coat. He would find her and bring her home. She would see reason; she always did eventually, for he possessed the power to bend people to his will, especially Valarie.

One day, she would thank him for it.

Outside Delmonico's, Scrooge stood and watched his former self stride purposefully down the crowded sidewalk, gradually merging into the anonymous throng.

He heaved a sigh of relief, grateful to have been released from that unbearable nightmare. The distant thunder of angry words reverberated in his head, accusations, justifications, and recriminations, the Unholy Trinity of a broken world.

She had resisted him, but at a terrible price. According to Leah, the overdose had not been a cry for help, but a desperate attempt to be heard above the yelling and screaming that had become their life.

He had ignored the signs. Losing the baby was an accident, not his fault. She miscarried. He carried on. What else could he do?

They separated soon after, and he had heard nothing from her since. Until tonight, that was. Now she had the child she craved, and he?

He heaved a sigh of relief.

"Thank God that's over."

"Accusations, justifications, and recriminations."

The words splashed against his face like icy water.

"What?"

He turned around, half expecting to see Jake standing in the shadows.

A yellow taxicab was parked alongside him, its passenger door wide open. He didn't recall summoning one, but wasn't going to look a gift horse in the mouth. Not tonight anyway. Something about the cabbie looked familiar. Who wears a peaked cap and shades in the evening?

"Taxi, sir?"

"Do I know you?" inquired Scrooge, "you look familiar."

"I doubt you know me," said the cabbie in an accent Scrooge found difficult to place, "but I know you, Ebenezer."

Scrooge was offended by the man's impertinence, but he said nothing. Something about the guy gave him the creeps.

"It was a shame she lost your baby," said the cabbie.

"She miscarried," blurted Scrooge, "it was just one of those unfortunate things."

How did this guy know? Who was he, and why did Scrooge suddenly feel as guilty as sin?

The taxi driver said nothing, just stared as Scrooge shuffled uncomfortably from one foot to the other.

"I don't have to justify myself to you," declared Scrooge vehemently. "Who the hell do you think you are anyway?"

"For now, Ebenezer, I am your guide," pronounced the taxi driver.

Scrooge snorted his contempt.

"My guide, huh? Well, there's plenty of other guides available for hire," Scrooge observed sarcastically, "we call them cabbies."

"None of those others can take you where you need to go, Ebenezer."

The taxi driver looked across the street, and Scrooge followed his gaze. A neon sign announced the latest movie attraction - '*Ghost*' starring Patrick Swayze, Demi Moore, and Whoopi Goldberg.

Scrooge realised he had no choice unless he wished to remain trapped in his own past. The taxi driver gestured towards the taxi. The door is still wide open.

"Get in," ordered the cabbie.

Scrooge clambered in and shut the door firmly, as if in so doing he could finally exorcise the images from his past.

"Take me to the Starwebs' building."

"Hold tight."

He was totally unprepared for what happened next.

This was how those astronauts must feel when the shuttle surges off the launch pad, and the G-force compresses their bodies into their seats.

A kaleidoscope of coloured light flowed past the window, an electric river in flood.

"For God's sake, man, slow down, what are you trying to do, kill us?"

"You don't escape that easily, Ebenezer."

It took a monumental effort, but Scrooge managed to turn his head enough to catch sight of the driver.

He was clad in a blue uniform, his face obscured by the incongruous shades. With difficulty, Scrooge ignored the presumptuous informality.

"You're not a cabbie. Who are you? Where are you taking me?"

Wherever it was, it could not possibly be worse than the horrors he had already endured.

"A party, Ebenezer. We all know how you love parties. But a little detour first."

Scrooge felt he had been suddenly transported into the middle of a science fiction movie. Only this character came equipped with a heavy dose of sarcasm.

The taxi, or whatever this contraption was, had come to a halt. Scrooge gazed out of the window in a frantic attempt to reorient himself. The question was not only *where* he was, but also *when* he was.

The scene outside looked vaguely familiar if you had ever lived in the suburbs. They all looked pretty much the same. It was dark, and he did not recognise the street. It seemed ludicrous to think that he had been grateful to Doug for lending them the money to put a deposit on a nondescript place like these.

Doug had been like an overgrown puppy, just wanting to please. Scrooge remembered how fond he had been of Valarie, of them both. It was just as well Doug had not been around for the split and its consequent fallout. He resolved to remain in his seat, whatever happened.

"Where are we?"

"Can't you guess?"

"That's not . . ."

Scrooge was unable to complete the sentence.

"Your old house? Yes," confirmed his guide.

"I'm not going inside," insisted Scrooge.

It was a place where too many memories lay in wait.

"This night it is no longer within your power to refuse anything, Ebenezer, but you need not fear, this is not your home anymore."

The cabbie spoke with an air of authority that no power on earth could countermand.

"Do you remember how excited Doug was when you moved in?"

"Yeah," recalled Scrooge with an affection that took him by surprise, "like an overgrown puppy. He insisted I carry Val over the threshold."

The memory was bittersweet.

"He lent us the money. I can't believe I was so excited about moving into such a dump."

"Doug had such high hopes for you both."

"Yeah, well, Doug always was a glass-half-full kind of guy," observed Scrooge as though diagnosing an ailment.

"It's a blessing he died before you and Valarie broke up," the taxi driver observed.

"I guess so," responded Scrooge, "never figured it that way before."

Suddenly, the passenger door jerked open, and the taxi driver was standing on the sidewalk looking in at Scrooge.

"I wish you'd stop doing stuff like that," Scrooge protested.

"Come, time is short."

Scrooge stepped out of the taxi and found himself not on the sidewalk, but in the hallway of his former home. Apart from the décor, nothing had changed.

"Houses store memories just like people," said his guide, "do you have memories, Ebenezer?"

The Same Hallway, June 1990

Scrooge set down his briefcase in the hallway. Valarie was seated at the foot of the stairs, in her hand a glass, and by her side a half-empty bottle. She watched him take off his coat and hang it slowly and deliberately on the hall stand. A smile flickered briefly across her face like a half-remembered tune.

"Welcome home, Benny darling," she said, raising her glass in a mocking gesture.

"Sorry, dinner's not ready. I've been a little busy."

"You're drunk," he replied, "again."

"Can't a girl have a bit of fun once in a while?" she replied, attempting to mimic a spoilt child, but her slurred words betrayed her.

"You never used to mind."

"What about the baby?" said Scrooge, turning to face her.

"Why the sudden concern about Megan?" she asked, making it sound more like an accusation.

"Megan?" responded Scrooge, suddenly concerned that Valarie was apparently bonding with her child so early in her pregnancy. It was not what he had anticipated.

"It's a Welsh name," she explained as though he were interested, "didn't you know some of my family came from Wales, Benny?"

She paused, inviting a response, but none came.

"There's a lot you don't know about me, Benny, or couldn't be bothered to find out more like."

She took another sip of her drink.

"Too busy with all that important business, I guess."

Scrooge was becoming tired of her maudlin self-pity.

"How can you tell it's a girl?" he said, "It's far too early in the pregnancy."

Valarie smirked.

"Don't tell me you've been reading up on it like a proud expectant father?"

The smirk disappeared, and her lower lip began to tremble, but she struggled to remain in control.

"Trust me, Benny, it's a girl, alright, a mother can sense these things."

She stood unsteadily, and Scrooge took a step towards her, but she stopped him with a gesture of her hand.

"I've got the start of a headache," she said half to herself, "I'm going to have a lie down."

She began to climb the stairs. She had almost reached the top when Scrooge called after her.

"I've booked an appointment at the clinic."

Valarie froze.

A truck roared past outside, and Scrooge listened as it faded into silence.

Valarie slowly turned round to face him.

"You are one hell of a sensitive son of a bitch, you know that, Benny?"

Valarie was not slurring now.

"You can stick your appointment where the sun don't shine, I'm not going."

Her eyes blazed defiance, but Scrooge pressed on.

"We talked about this already," he reminded her, "and came to a decision. Now isn't a good time for us."

"Us!" screamed Valarie. "What 'us'?"

"We'll talk about it later when you've sobered up," he said, bending over to pick up the briefcase, signalling the end of the 'conversation'.

"It's for the best."

"Best for who, Benny?" she yelled, lifting the bottle above her head.

"To hell with you and your 'best'."

Scrooge stepped aside, and the bottle smashed against the front door, trailing splashes of red wine over the carpet. But in the act of throwing, Valarie lost her footing and tumbled headlong down the stairs.

"Valarie!" he cried as her body thumped heavily against each step before coming to rest, seemingly lifeless at his feet.

The red wine framed her like fresh splatters of blood.

He knelt beside her crumpled form and shook her gently. There was no response. Fighting back the panic, he stood, took out his mobile phone, and dialled 911.

"I need an ambulance, quickly."

Scrooge stood and looked down at the carpet where she had lain. The stains were gone, so was the carpet, and so was Valarie.

"Well, Ebenezer?" inquired the cabbie. "Any memories?"

"Can't say I have," replied Scrooge, still staring at the floor.

The cabbie regarded him for a long time, and Scrooge was beginning to feel distinctly uncomfortable, when a woman suddenly appeared at the head of the stairs.

Scrooge stepped back a pace, sighing with relief when he realised it was not Valarie. It was a woman Scrooge had never seen before.

"Have no fear, Ebenezer," said the taxi driver in that quaint old-fashioned way of his, "she cannot see or hear you."

The woman ascended the stairs and walked across the hallway into what used to be the lounge. The Taxi driver followed and beckoned Scrooge to do the same. Scrooge is once again staring fixedly at the floor.

"Come, Ebenezer, time is short," said his guide.

Scrooge turned away and followed the Spirit into the lounge.

His guide stood at the foot of a bed in the centre of the room, facing the window. A small child of about three or four years lay there, motionless. The woman was now sitting on the edge of the bed, stroking the child's hair and occasionally bending forward to kiss the boy's forehead. He was not asleep, for his eyes were open and fixed intently upon Scrooge.

"He can see me."

The thought disturbed him profoundly, but he could not say why.

"The thought troubles you, Ebenezer? Do not be troubled, you and I are invisible to mortal eyes. Yet," the creature weighed its words carefully, "young children often possess the power to pierce the veil and gaze into our realm, for they are as yet uncorrupted by the world."

If that little speech was meant to offer reassurance to Scrooge, it had the opposite effect. References to 'veil' and 'realm' did nothing to quell the turbulent waves of panic crashing against his skull.

The child lowered his eyes as though the effort of keeping them open had drained him of strength. It was only then that Scrooge noticed the I.V. line inserted in the child's arm.

"What's wrong with him?"

His companion did not answer, and at that moment the woman took a glass of water from a bedside table and handed it to the child. Even the act of smiling appeared an effort, and he sipped the water without speaking.

"Daddy shouldn't be long now. Try to get some sleep. You know who's coming tonight."

The child closed his eyes, but whether this was in response to his mother's prompting or the inevitable consequence of his weakened condition, Scrooge couldn't tell. The mother watched the child for a moment before leaning over and kissing him on the forehead.

The front door slammed, and she lifted her head.

Into the room rushed a figure still clad in his snow-dusted coat. She rose and placed a finger on her lips. The man looked crestfallen.

"I was hoping to get back before he went to sleep."

He looked vaguely familiar, and suddenly recognition dawned upon Scrooge. Scratchitt! The guy who'd tried to pull a fast one with the holidays earlier. Why were they in Scratchitt's house?

"That's Scratchitt," declared Scrooge, "don't tell me that loser bought my house?"

His companion did not answer, and Scrooge lapsed into a morose silence.

"What kept you?"

There was a hint of mild admonition in her voice.

"Or should I say, who kept you?"

Scratchitt shifted uneasily on his feet and fidgeted with the brim of his hat. Scrooge noticed he did not look at his wife when he answered.

"He's a busy guy, Ellen. Running a huge corporation and everything. He saw me eventually."

"Yeah, he's a regular guy all right. Why do you always do that, Bob?"

She glanced at the child, conscious that she had raised her voice. He did not stir.

Seizing the moment, her husband stepped forward and embraced her in a bear-like hug. She stiffened at first, then her face broke into a smile that seemed to light up the room.

"I've got the extra week."

In response to what Scrooge felt was hardly news of global significance, his wife whooped with delight.

"Well, God Bless Mr Scrooge!"

He had definitely missed something.

Together, they sat down by the side of the bed. Scrooge noted he had failed to mention the two weeks he would lose in the summer.

"He's H.I.V. Positive"

Scrooge jumped. He had almost forgotten the creature was there. Something about the scene before him held a fascination he could not explain.

"You mean Aids?"

Instinctively, he took a step backwards. Had he shaken hands with the guy earlier? He was almost certain he hadn't, almost.

"You have nothing to fear from this child, Ebenezer."

Embarrassment flushed Scrooge's cheeks.

"How long has he got?"

"Not long. This may be his last Christmas."

"Is there nothing they can do?"

"There are medications that could prolong his life for many years, but they are expensive and beyond the means of this family."

"Even if they could, I suppose it would only delay the inevitable."

"If that were true, Ebenezer, I would not be here."

The creature turned towards him, and though he could not see its face behind the shades, he felt the intensity of its scrutiny burn deep.

"Are you telling me the child can be cured?"

Scrooge knew that it was impossible, the cynicism in his voice betraying his lack of faith.

"When you love Ebenezer, every second is precious, every minute, every hour, every day, and every year. Love keeps its own time. Have you never loved Ebenezer?"

It was a question he could or would not answer. Not now, not ever. Instead, he did what he did best and took the offensive.

"That must have been tough?"

"Tough?"

It worked. The creature sounded confused.

"Well, you know, adopting a kid only to find it has Aids."

There followed a silence, and Scrooge could not conceal the sense of satisfaction he always felt when his words found their mark.

"Ah! I had forgotten how much store you earthbound creatures place on creed and colour. You misunderstand Ebenezer. They chose the child because of his affliction."

"They chose a kid because he had Aids?"

If this had been a boxing match, Scrooge had just been hit with a sucker punch.

"Do you now understand what you have missed? They chose to love even though they knew it would be the source of both great pain and great joy. That is the most precious kind of love, Ebenezer. Come, my hour is nearly done."

He was reluctant to leave, but the creature gave him no choice. It seized Scrooge by the arm and led him to the door. Scrooge glanced back quickly over his shoulder at the child on the bed. This time, the child did not open its eyes, and Scrooge experienced a tug of disappointment.

They stepped into the hallway where a modest Christmas tree sparkled and glittered, joyfully defiant of the dark. The creature opened the front door, and Scrooge was propelled out into the street.

PART 4
The Conclusion

Outside Starwebs Inc.

He stumbled, striking his knees on the sidewalk. The taxi was waiting, but he was no longer outside Scratchitt's house. He stood and gazed upwards. The Starwebs Inc. building reached into the night sky as though grasping at the cold, indifferent stars, bathing him in its monstrous shadow.

"See Ebenezer, you have built your tower toward the heavens, but what name have you made for yourself?"

The creature moved towards the taxi, and Scrooge made to follow, but it held up a gloved hand.

"Farewell, Ebenezer. Someone waits for you."

Scrooge recalled a line of verse:

"Like one who on a lonesome road doth walk in fear and dread,

And having once turned round walks on, and no more turns his head,

Because he knows a frightful fiend doth close behind him tread."

And immediately wished he hadn't. He watched the taxi until it was swallowed up by the hollow dark streets, not because of any sentimental attachment to his late companion, but because, like the man on that lonesome road, he also did not wish to turn round.

This was nonsensical. Whatever had happened to him tonight, this was still New York City, and he was still one of its most powerful denizens. There was nothing he need fear. Nothing! Yet he was afraid. Worse, he was vulnerable.

Emotions buried long ago stirred deep within, fresh shoots breaking through the dead ground of a barren field.

"Someone waits for you."

He sensed its presence behind him, and with grim determination, he turned to face whatever being had passed through the eternal veil into the world of men.

A little girl with auburn hair stood at the top of the steps, looking down at him. She was dressed in the pink party dress he recalled her wearing earlier that evening. Their eyes met briefly, then she turned and walked towards the building, vanishing from sight.

Overwhelmed by a sudden and irresistible need to confront the child, he raced up the steps. At the top, he paused to regain his breath and make a mental note to have serious words with his personal fitness coach.

There was no sign of the girl with auburn hair. There was no sign of anyone. Security was conspicuous by its absence.

He moved cautiously towards the entrance as though approaching an alien edifice of unknown origin. A portal to strange new worlds, where he was unsure, he would be welcomed with open arms.

The foyer was deserted. Only the Christmas tree, festooned with a myriad twinkling lights, lit the gloom like distant constellations.

A sudden breeze blew through the tree, and a hail of baubles fell and shattered around him. The tree lights flickered, dimmed, and died. Scrooge needed no light. He knew the way. She had shown him earlier.

When he got to the lift, it was already in use, as he knew it would be. He watched its progress upwards until it stopped at the floor that housed his private hospitality suite, where many lucrative deals had been struck with some of the world's most influential and powerful individuals.

It should not have been possible for the child to have accessed this level, but this was no ordinary child. This was no ordinary night.

He waited for the lift to descend. When it did, he stepped inside. It was empty. The doors closed, and he ascended. It stopped where he knew it would, and the doors slid apart.

The hallway was also empty. There was no sign of the child. He debated whether he should return to the level below where normality beckoned, but in truth, the decision had already been taken by a far Senior Executive, and no alternative option was open to him.

He stepped out into the hallway and walked slowly towards the Hospitality Suite. The suite was in use. Someone from Security stood sentinel outside the door, his massive arms folded in the classic universal pose that marked their breed.

Scrooge's brow furrowed; he had given no authorisation for its use. Perhaps now the orchestrator of this bizarre conspiracy would at last reveal himself. Scrooge yet clung to the forlorn hope that the evening had been somehow ingeniously contrived by, as yet, a person, or persons unknown.

Anger, born of the humiliating experiences he had been forced to endure this dreadful evening, surged through his body, and he seized the handle of the door with aggressive intent. Immediately, massive fingers closed around his wrist with such force that pins and needles pierced his hand, and he began to lose feeling in his arm.

"Your invite, please, sir."

"Don't you recognise me, you jackass? I'm Ebenezer Clinton Scrooge III."

The guard held Scrooge tight, his bulk still barring the way.

"I don't have an invite, and tomorrow you won't have a job," threatened Scrooge.

"No one gets in without an invitation. Check your jacket pocket, please, Sir."

"What!" declared Scrooge angrily.

The impassive voice exuded authority that Scrooge calculated no force on earth could deny.

The Sentinel motioned towards Scrooge's jacket at the same time releasing his grip. Scrooge rubbed his hand ruefully, but discretion advised him not to make any further issue of the matter. Instead, he submissively reached inside his jacket and felt the hard corner of a card that he was sure had not been there before.

"Wait, this is for a child's party."

"Correct, this is your personal invitation. It has your name on it."

It was gilt-edged with two balloons in the left-hand corner, one red and one blue. Written upon it in a child's hand was just one word, *Papa*.

The universe imploded, and he felt his very being sucked into a dark, swirling vortex from which there would be no way back. He leaned against the wall to steady himself and felt the invitation plucked from his hand.

"This seems in order, sir. You had better go in, everyone is waiting for you," said the guard standing aside.

The door opened, and Scrooge stepped into the maelstrom. The hospitality suite was a large room, admittedly, but the scene before him defied logic.

He recalled a time in the orphanage when Miss Stryker had left her hand mirror on his dressing table. He had picked it up and turned it towards the mirror, so that the images seemed to repeat themselves endlessly into infinity. How he had longed to be able to step into one of those alternative universes, but it was merely an illusion, and fate bound him irrevocably to the reality that remained.

Before him, the room stretched away impossibly towards a lost horizon. In its centre, around a table adorned with countless balloons, were seated a host of children as numerous as the distant stars.

Their faces, illuminated by an inner light, were turned towards him as if his arrival had been long anticipated. He stood transfixed as they continued to stare at him, radiant with an innocence untainted by the world. It was like looking into the sun, and he tried desperately to avert his eyes, but he was held by their unwavering gaze that pierced to the very root of his being, laying him bare before them.

There was no condemnation in their expression, only compassion, yet he was filled with a nameless fear and dread, as must a condemned man who faces his executioner and the final judgment beyond.

As though part of one single entity, the children turned away, and the moment passed. For the first time, Scrooge noticed that sat next to each child was an adult wearing an expression of mingled wonder and awe similar, he realised, to the one he probably now wore.

A small hand slipped into his own. The child with auburn hair stood before him.

"I'm so glad you came, Papa."

It was a name he had heard many times, but never before directed at him. Valarie had always called her late father Papa. Scrooge had never known him. He died shortly before he and Valarie had first met, but she spoke of him often with a fondness that Scrooge found irritating, and which aroused within him an emotion he refused to acknowledge.

Why should he be jealous of any man? Especially someone who no longer existed. Yet it was this very fact that irked him.

Death had placed him beyond Scrooge's reach, and from beyond the grave he had presided over their marriage like a cheap plaster saint. Every perceived indiscretion was sufficient for Valarie to invoke his presence, and inevitably, Scrooge would fall far short of the exalted standards he had set.

Any attempt to discredit his memory only intensified the aura surrounding it. Was it possible that this child…

"Who are you?"

He tried in vain to keep his voice steady. The touch of her hand was unbearably distracting. Something was stirring deep within him, something he had locked away a lifetime ago and banished from his consciousness. Now it had been summoned forth by a child's fragile touch.

"Oh, Papa."

"Papa," he repeated, "It's what you used to call your father. Did you know I was jealous of him?" he continued, conscious he was babbling. "I could never live up to his exalted standards in your eyes, but I never stopped loving you, Valarie."

She laughed as a child does when teased. Tugging gently at Scrooge, she led him to the head of the table where two vacant chairs awaited them. He sat down, unable to avert his eyes from her face.

Her face, for the second time this night, he looked upon the face he had never stopped loving. Her blue eyes held his own, and a sudden cold wind embraced his body. Valarie's eyes were green.

"Valarie?"

"I'm not Valarie, silly, Valarie is Mama's name."

"Then who are you?"

But even as he spoke the words, he knew the answer, for it was branded upon his forehead like the mark of Cain.

"Can't you guess?"

"Megan?"

Megan. It was the name Valarie had chosen in deference to her Welsh ancestry, of which she was inordinately proud. For once, he let her have her way. What did it matter anyway? The child would never be born. It had proved a serious error of judgment for the very act of naming the child bestowed on Valarie a moral strength he never imagined she possessed. From then on, she resisted him at every turn, but the effort drained her vitality, and she sought refuge in drink.

The miscarriage had been a fortuitous consequence.

"That's impossible. Valarie lost our child."

Even now, he refused to speak her name. Even now, he refuses to accept his portion of the blame.

"Nothing that has ever lived is truly lost, Papa."

She looked at him, and the revelation of what he had lost swept over him, a chill wind announcing the onset of a long and bitter winter.

Images of what might have been flashed through his mind, and he tried to grasp hold of them, but they evaded him like autumn leaves scattered in a sudden storm.

He bowed his head, unable to look at her, unable to look his Megan in the face.

A hand touched his cheek, brushing away a solitary, bemused tear, lost on the unfamiliar terrain.

"Why me? Why not your mother? She grieved for a long time."

"I know. But Mama doesn't need to see me; she always keeps me close here."

Megan placed a hand across her chest.

"What do you want from me?"

He was ready now, ready to pay any price to end his torment, but Megan did not answer.

"What do you want me to do, Megan?"

"Set him free, Papa."

"Who? Set who free? I don't understand!"

It was he who needed release. His head spun. The still waters of his subconscious had been disturbed, and raw emotion clouded his thoughts.

"You must come with me, Papa."

Megan stood and, taking him firmly by the hand, led him towards the door. He turned back for one last look, but although the table still stretched toward an unknown destination, no one was seated there.

The guests had silently departed.

"Who was the party for?" he asked as he embraced the scene one last time.

"It was mine, Papa."

He turned sharply in response to Megan's voice, which had suddenly deepened and mellowed.

A young woman stood before him. A beautiful young woman with auburn hair and blue eyes. Eyes that regarded him with a sorrowful solemnity.

"I would have been eighteen today."

He recoiled from the import of her words, at the sudden revelation of all that might have been.

"Christmas Eve. Megan, I am so very sorry."

"Papa, listen!"

He was stilled before the urgency and authority of her voice and bearing.

"You do not need to be sad for me, but for you, there is so little time. Come."

She led him by the hand, out into the hallway. The Sentinel was no longer at his post. They turned right, and Scrooge knew immediately where they were going.

He struggled to keep pace with her, and when at last she stopped outside the Presentation Suite, he took time to catch his breath.

"You know this place?" she asked.

"Yes," he replied, "I know this place."

"You have influenced many people in this room, Papa."

It was a statement of fact. Scrooge did not ask how she knew.

"Oh yes," he replied, "I've done a lot of business in there."

"Doesn't it make you feel proud?" inquired Megan.

"Not anymore," he replied, his voice barely above a whisper.

Megan took both his hands in her own and gazed into his eyes with an intensity.

"You must go in alone."

"Will I see you again?"

The thought of losing her once more was almost too much to bear.

"That is no longer my choice."

His heart lifted as he realised she, too, felt pain at the prospect of parting.

"Papa, go!"

The urgency in her voice compelled him to action. The heavy panelled door towered ominously above him, and he reached forward tentatively as though contact with its polished surface were an act of hostile intent.

He paused and turned to her one last time, seeking reassurance and drawing strength from her presence, but she was gone. Driven by a grim resolve, he opened the door and entered.

Darkness enfolded him deeper than the night. Where were the lights? The lights were programmed to activate as soon as someone entered the room. He frantically struggled to compose himself, but the events of the night were persistent intruders, disrupting his attempts to think logically. Gradually, he formed an image in his mind of the suite's layout.

The central sector of the room was arranged like a mini-cinema, but instead of a single screen, a multitude of large monitors had been assembled, giving the appearance of a single immense screen.

Each monitor represented a different satellite channel owned and controlled by Starwebs Inc. It was a persuasive tool in the hands of a master manipulator. Once a prospective client realised just how much influence and control could be exerted through these portals, they were practically begging to be allowed to conclude a deal on whatever terms Scrooge cared to propose.

He had just about fumbled his way to the seats without causing himself any damage when the screens activated spontaneously, and the darkness reluctantly slunk back into the shadows, gathering in black pools around the room's perimeter. Scrooge found the nearest chair and sat down heavily, his heart hammering hard against his chest.

"Ebenezer Scrooge, you have been weighed in the scales and found wanting."

Scrooge sprang to his feet. The voice had come from behind.

He was obviously not alone.

Was there someone seated in the back row, or was it merely a manifestation of his feverishly overburdened imagination?

"Who's there?"

"What do you want?"

He peered intently into the gloom, but the shadows flickered and shifted deceptively as an image on the screen began to grow and take shape.

"Starwebs Incorporated International regrets to announce the death of their CEO and distinguished leader Ebenezer Clinton Scrooge III, following a brief illness."

Scrooge spun round, facing the screen, and stepped forward, drawn like a moth to its shimmering brightness.

Looming over him was the figure of Ed Burgh, the network's premier anchor man. Each monitor displayed a different part of Ed's anatomy, like some gigantic digital jigsaw assembled for this single purpose. Impossibly white teeth flashed briefly as he spoke in appropriately low sombre tones.

"Although head of arguably the most powerful and influential media empire on the planet, Ebenezer Scrooge ironically shied away from the glare of publicity. Such was his passion for privacy that he famously refused to give an interview to Forbes magazine and was rarely seen in public. It is rumoured that after the late Princess Diana, his was the most prized scalp coveted by the now infamous paparazzi."

What the hell was this guy talking about? One thing is for sure: after next week, the only news he will be able to deliver will be from the front page of the Spare Change News on some downtown street corner.

Ed's image was replaced by that of Scrooge exiting the Ritz-Plaza Hotel flanked by security. He holds a magazine protectively to hide his face as photographers surround him. Flashes light the screen. As Scrooge is pictured getting into his limousine and speeding away, Ed Burgh continued his obituary.

"Although he mingled with presidents, world leaders, captains of industry and even royalty, Scrooge remained an enigma leading to frequent comparisons with Howard Hughes, probably the most famous recluse of modern times."

Images of Scrooge in the company of eminent celebrities and politicians flickered across the screen before the features of Ed Burgh reappeared like the Cheshire Cat.

"He was named Ebenezer, an apparent acknowledgement of his Jewish roots. His father survived the horrors of Dachau, although it is believed many of his family perished. . ."

Just like the Cheshire Cat, Ed Burgh disappeared without warning and was replaced with an older, grimmer image that Scrooge recognised immediately.

He stared at the black-and-white, grainy footage he knew so well. Footage he had privately viewed many times before. It had become a constant source of strength. Whenever difficult decisions needed to be taken in his personal or business life, he would turn to it and draw deeply from its bitter waters, which never failed to refresh his spirit and harden his resolve.

Now it loomed before him more terrible than ever.

"That's private footage, Burgh! You hear me! You're finished, you old hack."

Scrooge vented his impotent anger at the screen where a queue of people huddled together on a railway siding, alongside a row of cattle trucks. Men, women, and children carrying an assortment of baggage, under the watch of soldiers, moved slowly towards the open doors of the trucks.

Bemused children looked up at their parents for reassurance. They, in turn, struggled to suppress the fear and quell the panic mounting within as they offered what little comfort they could.

For Scrooge, it was akin to watching a Greek tragedy of epic proportions, in which one knows the fate that awaits the hero but is powerless to intervene and change his destined course.

Yet, this image had sustained him and made him strong. Never would a child of his enter this world powerless before the winds of fate or the whims of men.

That is what Valarie had failed to comprehend. It was not that he did not want the child; he did not want Megan ever to become a victim of capricious circumstance, as so many children had been. As he once was.

Looking at the images before him, could any man honestly deny that it would have been better if those children had never been born?

"Now do you understand, Megan?" pleaded Scrooge, "I couldn't let you into a world like this until I was strong enough to protect you."

Something in the image caught his eye. Something that had not been there before. A sudden surge of anger consumed him. Someone had tampered with his private footage, for amongst the many shades of grey he glimpsed a flash of colour.

It was a child's dress. The child, clutching a teddy bear, was looking around frantically. She had obviously been separated from her mother in the crowd and its relentless, driven march forward.

Her dress was pink. Her hair was auburn. She lifted her head and stared directly at him through pleading, frightened eyes, her face now filling the screen.

"Megan!"

It could not be. As he watched, she was pushed forward. The doors of the cattle truck were open, and people were being herded inside without dignity or compassion. Megan was roughly lifted into the arms of a soldier. Still, before he was able to discard her unceremoniously, two bare arms reached out and lifted her gently inside, and she disappeared into the shadows.

Yet it was not this unexpected act of compassion that caused Scrooge to bow his head and weep, as he had not wept since his own barren childhood. In her last moments, even as the soldier held her in his arms, she had turned to look directly at him, and she was smiling.

The image fragmented and was gone. In its place, the sombre countenance of Ed Burgh returned.

"Scrooge was born in New York City in February 1960. A new era was dawning for Americans, and a mood of optimism swept the country, but for Ebenezer Scrooge, a far darker destiny dogged the family's footsteps. In October of the following year, both his parents were tragically killed in an automobile accident when their car was hit by a truck, whose driver was proven to be heavily under the influence of alcohol."

A car, somewhere in New York State, 1966

Rain lashed against the windscreen with such fury that the wiper blades struggled to handle the volume of water. The woman glanced nervously at the driver as conditions deteriorated by the minute.

"Perhaps we should pull over till the storm blows itself out Joe," she suggested.

Her husband smiled, but kept his focus fixed firmly on the road ahead, which was becoming increasingly difficult to negotiate.

"You worry too much, honey," he reassured her.

"Let's get home before the kids wake up."

Scrooge's mother twisted round to look at the two children snuggled together on the back seat. The boy is asleep, leaning against his older sister. The girl looks up and smiles at her mother.

"You okay, Leah?" asks her mother. Leah nods.

"Keep an eye on Benny for me," she said.

The little girl is about to respond when the car judders, swerves towards the side of the road, and stops.

Their mother turned to her husband, consternation written across her face.

"What's wrong, Joe?"

Joe slapped his hands against the steering wheel in frustration.

"Tonight, of all nights," he sighed, "we get a flat."

Joe made to get out of the car, but his wife laid a restraining hand on his arm.

"Wait for the rain to ease, Joe, you'll get soaked."

"That could take all night," replied Joe, never the most patient of men.

Joe stepped out of the car to examine the tyre.

"Hold on, Joe," said his wife, "I have an umbrella."

She stepped out of the car, opened the umbrella, and held it over her husband, offering him what little protection she could from the elements.

Joe fumbled on his knees in the rain as the headlights of a truck appeared in the distance. They were both too concerned with finishing the job as quickly as possible, so they could get back into the shelter of the car, to notice that the oncoming vehicle was weaving erratically.

Christmas Eve was always a bitch, mused the truck driver as he took another swig of whiskey. He wiped his lips and tossed the empty bottle onto the seat beside him. Through the windscreen, an indistinct shape was just visible through the driving rain as the truck meandered a little too close to the centre of the road. Uttering a profanity, the driver swung the truck back the other way.

The headlights swept across the shape that was no longer indistinct, and now loomed large in front of him. The driver sees the car and the man and woman standing beside it too late. They are staring at him through wide, horrified eyes that have stared at him through a thousand cold-sweat nightmares.

"Holy crap!" he cried, pulling hard on the wheel to avoid hitting the car head-on.

There is a metallic scream as the truck scrapes against the length of the car and the dull thud of impact he once felt when he hit a deer. This was no deer.

Ed Burgh continued his remorseless monologue.

"With no immediate family to care for him, the infant Ebenezer Scrooge and his elder sister were placed in care. The infant Scrooge was sent to a state-run orphanage."

Outside the State Orphanage, 1972

Ezekiel Izzard stood on the opposite sidewalk and gazed up at a window on the second floor of the orphanage. He imagined the child sitting on the edge of the bed waiting for him. He was in no rush; he would take his time. This was his domain.

Flakes of snow drifted past the window as a child's face appeared and pressed itself against the glass.

Ezekiel stepped out of the glare of the streetlamp and into the shadows. He did not want the boy to see him. His visit would be a surprise; he liked it that way.

Snow was falling thicker now. Turning up his collar, he walked quickly across the street, his feet leaving a trail of black scars in the thickening snow.

He ascended the flight of stone steps worn down by the anonymous ghosts of past generations of lost children and opened the heavy wooden doors.

Standing in the hallway, he gazed up the flight of stairs shrouded in shadows before beginning his ascent.

The old wooden steps creaked and groaned under the weight of his passing. His breath came thick and heavy with anticipation as he stepped onto the landing on the second floor.

Light seeped from beneath the door.

The child heard the footsteps on the stairs as he watched the falling snow, which suddenly turned to dust and ashes. There was no escape. The window was firmly secured. He turned and flung himself on the bed, instinctively assuming the position that was a subconscious reminder of the security he had once known in his mother's womb.

Izzard stood outside the door and spoke low and soft, while the boy pressed his hands hard against his ears.

"You awake Ebenezer?"

There was no response.

"Don't try fooling me boy, I saw your face in the window."

Still only silence.

"Mrs Stryker tells me you've been a very naughty boy," he said. "That will not do, that will not do at all, Ebeneezer."

Ezekiel Izzard opened the door. The boy lay in a foetal position facing the wall with the rose-patterned wallpaper. Izzard stepped inside and closed the door behind him.

"Here he remained for the next sixteen years. Very little is known about this period of his life as he steadfastly refused to disclose any details. Speculation fuelled by the tabloid press following the investigation and subsequent convictions of many employees suspected of child abuse in state institutions cannot be categorically confirmed or denied.

What we can say is this, that Ebenezer Scrooge surmounted enormous personal tragedies and setbacks that would have discouraged most men."

Ed Burgh's teeth shimmered like the Northern Lights, then vanished. In his place, an enormous window appeared, viewed from the perspective of the interior of a room gloomy with shadows.

Through the window, street lamps briefly lit the twilight, illuminating the silhouettes of passersby, hurrying to keep pace with their silver breath as it snaked through the chill evening air.

He knew the room as intimately as any prisoner knows each stone of his solitary cell. He had been back there once before this evening and harboured no desire to return. Countless times, he had stood at this window and watched as parents with their children passed carelessly by on the other side. Their laughter seemed to beckon to him, and in his imagination, he would run outside and follow after them.

How he yearned to be allowed inside that closed circle called family, but they all disappeared into the distance before he could catch up with them, blissfully unaware he even existed.

The window drew closer, and Scrooge guessed he was now viewing the room through the occupant's eyes, the boy he had once been an eternity before. Two people were leaving the orphanage: a woman and a man. Which child, he wondered, would even now be experiencing the stinging slap of rejection?

What he would not have given to be walking down those steps between them, the touch of their hands upon his own; but he was never allowed out of his room when visitors called, for he was one of the 'special' children.

It was as the man stooped to enter the car that he caught sight of his face. On the screen before him, the boy pressed his face longingly against the windowpane, but Scrooge stepped back, suddenly filled with confusion. The young man's face had been his own. He sensed a revelation of great significance was within his grasp, but just as you reach out to touch your reflection in a still pool, it shattered, and was gone.

The voice of Ed Burgh once again reverberated inside his head.

"It was this indomitable spirit that enabled him to forge a media empire, informed observers believe, that influenced many of the major political decisions of our generation.

But, like all great men, he was not without his critics. The most strident voices alleged that Starwebs was deployed as a propaganda tool by governments worldwide, seeking to gain popular support for policies difficult to justify on moral grounds alone.

They commonly cite the devastating humanitarian cost of ensuing global conflicts that such policies allegedly ignited."

A plane screamed overhead, and suddenly, a group of naked children were running towards Scrooge, terror etched on their faces. Some screamed in pain, their bodies blistered and raw. One of the children appeared to be running straight at him, her arms outstretched, imploringly.

It was, he knew, merely an optical illusion, yet what compelled him to move towards the screen was the child's face. He recognised her at once and stretched out his arms to offer her refuge.

He swiftly withdrew his hands as a black cloud of flies, seemingly disturbed by his sudden movement, burst upwards, and, although he knew it to be merely an image, he involuntarily covered his mouth. The very thought of their defiling presence sickened him.

The screen cleared, and a child with enormous eyes and emaciated body stared up and through him, to a place beyond the suffering of this world. It was held in the arms of a skeletal creature he took to be its mother. She watched impassively as the flies returned and settled on the child's face. Neither mother nor child attempted to drive them away. He sensed they had both travelled far in search of food, and their journey had taken them past despair to that desolate place called Resignation.

The image receded, and he witnessed, from a great height, a ragged queue of humanity, lost in the shimmering heat of the desert. He dared not look too closely, for he feared that somewhere amongst that abandoned mass was a child with auburn hair.

The image blurred and was replaced with others. A kaleidoscopic display of horrors that numbed his senses until Scrooge felt he could bear no more.

Children with soulless expressions swaggered around with guns instead of toys—lost boys and girls who had never heard of Neverland—children filled with hate cast stones at soldiers.

By dusty roadsides, children begged for bread or sold themselves in filthy brothels.

"Please, enough!" Scrooge covered his face, but he could not block out the noise and the stench that assailed his other senses.

"But great men rise above the petulant criticism of their peers. Never once did Ebenezer Scrooge dignify these base charges with a response. His silence is an eloquent testimony that truth will stand on its own merits."

Scrooge groaned. Why didn't the man shut up?

"And you called us monsters."

It could not be. Scrooge spun around.

The room was no longer empty. Two figures clothed in shadow stood behind the back row of seats. He did not need to see their faces, for he had never been able to completely exorcise the sound of their voices from his head.

It was Stryker who had spoken.

"You were monsters. We were children. You were supposed to protect us."

"You never went hungry, did you, Ebenezer?"

"You always had clothes to wear."

"A warm bed to sleep in."

"Not like those children."

Izzard and Stryker spoke in turn—an infernal double act.

"Besides, we couldn't have been that bad."

"Else you would have left us long ago."

"What are you talking about? I did leave. "

"Did you, Ebenezer? Did you really?"

Stryker spoke in the matronly tones she loved to affect when about to discipline one of her charges. The fact that they were both dead brought little comfort.

Izzard had died suddenly and inexplicably in the street outside the orphanage years ago. The circumstances surrounding his death had never been fully explained. Stryker had apparently been heartbroken by his passing, and the last few years of her life were spent as a destitute alcoholic.

"You're both dead!" declared Scrooge.

"But not to you, Sonny, not to you."

As, once more, Scrooge stood helpless before them, they stepped back and were immediately swallowed by the dark.

"Even now, tributes to the life and accomplishments of Ebenezer Clinton Scrooge III are flooding in by the hour."

Ed Burgh would not be silenced, even by the dead.

"However, in keeping with his life, the funeral is expected to be a very private affair for close friends and family members only."

Assured that the shades of Izzard and Stryker no longer lurked in the shadows, Scrooge slumped in the front row and listened to the details of his funeral arrangements. It certainly would be a small gathering. Perhaps he should have taken Facebook more seriously.

Like a shark breaking through surface water, the shiny grill of a gleaming black hearse raced towards him. It was the first of a cortège of three that wound their way from Manhattan towards the Mount Hebron Cemetery, where the parents he could not remember had been laid to rest half a century before. Their remains were now housed in a private mausoleum, and it was here the cortège came to a halt.

The doors swung open, and he watched with growing apprehension to see who would emerge. Grainger, as dependable as a rock, was the first to alight and open the doors of the mourner's car.

Leah stepped out, shielding her face against the low winter sun. She was followed by another woman, whose auburn hair he glimpsed beneath her wide-brimmed hat. Valarie had come. He had not expected that, and he doubted he would have done the same if the roles had been reversed.

The third occupant was also a woman. He recognised her immediately, even though she kept repeatedly dabbing her eyes with a handkerchief, apparently overcome by the emotion of the occasion. It was Eva. He was surprised by the way her presence affected him. It was not just gratitude that she had elected to attend, but something deeper and more personal. There were just two occupants of the third. "Scratchitt!"

What on earth were Scratchitt and his wife doing there? What had he ever done for them? His thoughts fled back to the sick child in the bedroom. The way the wife had responded when told Scratchitt had been given an extended holiday.

"Love keeps its own time, Ebenezer."

So, he was not alone, but he did not care any more; a dam within him was cracking under the remorseless pressure of wasted years, swollen with regret and recriminations. He bowed his head, but he could not shut out the dark night that enveloped his soul.

"My brother was a solitary man. Not an easy man to know or love, so I thank you all for coming."

Leah was standing by the graveside, addressing the small gathering of mourners. Her voice drew him back from the void as she had so many years before.

"His had not been an easy life. We lost our parents when Benny was still a child. We grew up apart. I was lucky. A wonderful couple adopted me and made me their own. I assumed the same had happened to Benny.

When I eventually decided I wanted to find my brother, my parents supported me in every way possible. He was not living with a loving family as I had always imagined. All the happy carefree years I had spent growing up, he had spent in state institutions. He never talked about those years, and we never asked. Yet I have always carried a terrible sense of guilt that I did not look for him sooner, perhaps then. . ."

Leah paused to compose herself. No one stirred.

"No, Leah!"

Scrooge was on his feet now and moving towards her image on the screen.

"You saved me!"

But she could not hear him. No one could.

"We brought him home. My parents loved him as they had loved me. Yet it was as if a part of Benny never really left that dreadful place. I was too late."

Scrooge opened his mouth to protest once more, but the words died stillborn on his lips, for the truth was taking shape before him more terrible even than the shades of Stryker and Izzard.

"Then he met my dear friend Valarie, and I hoped. . . "

Her voice faded as she looked at Valarie, who bowed her head in response. Leah did not mention Megan by name, but she was there, as substantial as the air about them.

"After the divorce, Benny changed. He refused to see or speak with me. If it had not been for Eva, I would have lost him again. She read the letters he would not open, and never failed to reply."

Eva! He should feel angry and betrayed, yet he did not.

"The split between us hurt Stephen badly. He loved his uncle as much as I did. Being a single Mom is not easy, and I admit that I felt a sense of relief when he joined the army.

" She faltered, and the silence hung heavy.

"He would have been here today, I'm sure, if he had known. But I don't know where he is, or how to get in touch with him."

She stopped, and this time there was no carrying on.

Valarie stood and hurried forward to comfort her friend. The service was over.

The image blurred, and when it refocused, there was no sign of the others. He noticed that while Leah wore black, Valarie was in grey. Time had obviously passed. Leah was holding a bunch of roses, and they were standing next to a monument of some sort, but Scrooge was only able to see the base. It bore his name.

Ebenezer Clinton Scrooge III

"Benny"

1960 – 2010

"Thank you for coming. You have good reason to hate him."

"After losing Megan, I hated him more than anything in the world. But hate is so tiring, Leah. I couldn't keep it up forever. Besides, although I never knew her, I felt so close to Megan. I still do. Then I met Mike, and the rest, as they say, is history."

She glanced at the inscription as though to emphasise the point. Is that all he had become in the end, a turned page in someone's life?

"But what about you, Leah. Still no word from Stephen?"

There was concern in her voice as she drew closer.

"None. It's been over a year now. He left just before Benny died. I wrote to Benny, hoping Stephen might come looking for him."

Valarie threw her arms around her friend.

"Don't give up, Leah. I almost did, but there's always hope. Always."

She turned to the monument, attempting to distract Leah from her dark thoughts.

"I was kinda surprised by the choice, Leah. I thought you might have gone for angels."

"All those years alone in that place, he must have felt the world had abandoned him."

Valarie's eyes widened with understanding.

"That's him? That's Ebenezer."

She stood back, and Scrooge was given a clear view of the object in question.

A small boy sat on what appeared to be the corner of a bed. His head was turned away to his right. The likeness was uncanny, the pose all too familiar.

Scrooge knew exactly where the stone boy would gaze down the long, cold years. Not at the hard grey skies, but out through an old wooden window, suspended in time, to the indifferent world that lay beyond.

Leah leaned forward and placed the roses at the feet of the stone child. He noticed that dead flowers were scattered around like a carpet of remembrance. This was not the first time Leah had visited this place.

"I will not forget him again, Valarie. Not as long as I have breath in my body. I was too late to save the child, and that's why I lost the man."

She turned to her friend, tears flowing freely.

"I am so sorry, Val, that my failure brought you so much pain."

They embraced without speaking. Scrooge watched them walk slowly away arm in arm until he could see them no more.

A sudden breeze rustled the dead flowers like a whispered prayer. A petal lifted upwards, caught the passing wind, and Scrooge reached out impulsively to grasp it. When he opened his hand, it was there, moist and dark like a scarlet tear.

"No, Leah, forget the dead, forget me. Find Stephen. Bring him home."

"But 'New York is infested with such hopeless individuals seeking solace and oblivion in alcohol or drugs, authors of their own destruction, and as such deserving of no sympathy or special favours.'"

The voice again. Its source, he sensed, stood close behind him, and it could read his innermost thoughts. More than this, it had recorded them on some eternal ledger and preserved them as evidence to damn his soul. His thoughts reached out to Leah and

Valarie, to the hurt he had brought into their lives, and was still bringing.

And what of the hurt his actions had caused others? He stood guilty as condemned. His punishment would be just. Words recently spoken shed an unexpected light on his troubled spirit.

"There is always hope."

Was it possible, even now?

He resolved to face his accuser and plead forgiveness. For an instant, he glimpsed the outline of a commanding figure bathed in a pure light that did not hurt his eyes, but obscured his vision.

The figure pointed toward the doors. Scrooge thought he could discern the outline of enormous, folded wings. The creature moved within a radiant light, or maybe light emanated from its very being; he could not tell. One thing was certain: it would countenance no contradiction, and Scrooge was bound to obey its gestured command.

He moved slowly towards the door with the doleful tread of the condemned, and passed beyond.

"Mr Scrooge, you look absolutely dreadful. Can I get you a drink?" Eva hesitated. "Water is probably your best bet."

The sight of Eva flapping around him like a startled hen was not the scene he had expected. He nodded humbly, giving himself time to gather his thoughts. It seemed he was in the reception area outside the boardroom, not in the ante-room to the afterlife.

He approached the door, knocking loudly with his fist, unaware that Eva had returned with his glass of water and was now standing behind him, open-mouthed.

"See that Eva, real mahogany."

He rapped it again as if confirming his initial diagnosis.

"Yes, real mahogany. It's been like that for as long as I can remember. Are you feeling alright, Mr Scrooge?"

Eva was obviously struggling to contain her growing sense of alarm.

"What day is it, Eva?"

"What day?"

He obviously expected a serious answer, judging by the earnest expression on his face. She was becoming seriously concerned.

"Well, in another five minutes it will be Christmas Day," she said, "you know, jingle bells and all that stuff? Though your bells seem to be jingling pretty good right now."

Scrooge ignored Eva's flippancy.

"Five minutes. Then it's not too late! Sit down, Eva, we have work to do."

He had to be kidding. Only Scrooge could expect someone to work right up until Christmas Day. He probably spent his spare time squeezing the juice out of prunes. Why had she stayed with him so long? It was as if he read her mind.

"Why haven't you gone home yet?"

"I was worried about you."

She was about to qualify the statement, but realised she was blushing and scrabbled in her desk for a notepad.

"Yes, you have been, haven't you?"

His words implied more than was suggested by the immediate circumstances. Eva shifted uncomfortably and attempted to strike a professional pose.

"Have I ever commented on how attractive you are, Eva?"

"Most certainly not!"

He must have been drinking. Or was he laughing at her? She had thought he was oblivious to the fact that she was fond of him, well, actually, more than fond. Now he was cruelly playing with her affections. She resolved to maintain her composure, do her job, and go home. Maybe it was time for a change. New Year, new start.

"I thought so."

There was a note of regret in his voice she found disconcerting.

"Well, I should have."

Before she could respond, he rapidly changed the subject.

"Eva, I want you to write a memo to wire Scratchitt in the New Year."

"Scratchitt?" she queried.

"You know," he said, "the heavyweight I saw earlier."

She remembered the man he had kept waiting for so long.

"You mean Cratchitt, not Scratchitt."

Sounds like the guy was in deep trouble. Only Scrooge would contemplate firing someone on Christmas Eve. Happy New Year, Bobby!

"That's him, the one with the sick kid."

Eva shook her head. A sick kid to boot. It just keeps getting better and better.

"Tell him to take the year off, with pay. In fact, tell him I'm going to triple his salary."

Eva put down the pen and gave Scrooge a hard stare. This was going too far. If he wanted to mess with people's heads, he could do it himself.

"You serious?"

The tone in her voice suggested she had already worked out the answer for herself, and it was not one she approved of. Scrooge looked her in the eye, and her reservations evaporated. There was something in them she had never seen before, or expected to see ever, compassion and maybe even regret.

"Eva, I have never been more serious in my life. Oh, and find his address for me, I want to pay him a visit in the New Year."

It was becoming more difficult by the second to maintain a professional demeanour.

"Got it."

She kept her response short, not wanting him to detect the tremor in her voice. Eva began to write in her notebook.

"Is that all?"

"Hold it, Eva, one more thing," he added.

Eva stopped writing, and her demeanour became suddenly cold and distant.

"And what is this 'one more thing' exactly?" she inquired.

He paused as though uncertain of what to say next. She never thought she would see the day when Scrooge was lost for words.

"I want you to ring my sister."

"Leah! What, tonight? Don't you realise the time? She'll be asleep. Besides, you haven't spoken to her in years"

Scrooge had not realised how close Eva and his sister had become until hearing the protective edge in her voice.

"I'm sorry. That's none of my business."

Scrooge looked at her in a way that suggested he knew it was her business and had been for some considerable time.

"We both know she won't be asleep tonight, Eva, and we both know why?"

He smiled as a look of consternation crossed her face.

"I read her letter. The one you left by the bottle of Scotch. Guess you know me better than I do myself."

Eva's response was unexpected. She opened the desk drawer and rummaged around frantically, but to no avail; there was no letter.

"What letter?"

What could he tell her? That some being from the Other Side had been responsible? She was concerned enough about him already without bringing his sanity into question. He determined to ignore her confusion and press on.

"Just tell her I'm coming for dinner tomorrow and I will have two guests with me."

Eva raised her eyebrows and leaned back in the chair. She eyed him coolly.

"You do realise Christmas dinner is kinda special, Mr Scrooge. She might need a little more notice, don't you think?"

"Please call me Benny."

Eva looked like Alice must have when she landed at the bottom of the rabbit hole.

"Benny? Okay! And who shall I say is coming with you, Benny?"

His smile reminded her of a mischievous schoolboy, an analogy she would never have imagined applying to him.

"I would be honoured if you would accept my invitation to dinner, Eva. Before you object, we both know Leah would be delighted to have you."

"You mentioned two guests. Who is the other?"

He noted with satisfaction that she had not refused his invitation, merely delayed her acceptance.

"Stephen."

"Stephen? Leah's Stephen! You are kidding me. Leah doesn't even know where Stephen is."

She scrutinised his face carefully, trying to determine whether he was fooling around or genuinely losing the plot

"I know exactly where he is because I saw him earlier tonight. He's here in New York. I didn't recognise him at first. He's changed, and living on the streets hasn't helped."

He held back the part about having him forcibly removed. It was hard to come to terms with being truthful, though it felt somehow liberating. Telling the whole truth would be a different ball game altogether.

"But if he's living rough, how will you find him? It's a pretty big city, even with your resources, and I don't want to be the one to raise false hopes."

Scrooge ignored the sarcastic undertones.

"I'll find him tonight, and he will come home. Make the call, please, Eva."

She was accustomed to his arrogance. He was used to having his way. It came with the territory of being who he was. But it was not arrogance she saw reflected in his face, but a calm, unshakeable confidence as if he held a royal flush in a five-card hand of poker.

"And you expect me to wait around until you get back?"

He turned and smiled at her. It was funny how young he looked when he smiled. She smiled back. They both knew she had been waiting for him for years.

"Okay, I'll use one of the guest suites."

She watched him cross to the lift, where he paused and turned towards her.

"One last thing. The proposed new contract. Memo me to trash it."

Before she could protest and remind him of the inevitable repercussions, he had stepped into the lift. He was still smiling as the doors closed.

She dialled the number she knew so well. Leah answered as he said she would.

"Leah, it's me, Eva. No, there's nothing wrong, in fact quite the opposite. Leah, you'd better sit down "

He leant back against the steel wall of the lift and felt the weight of the years slip from his shoulders. A child was gazing up at him from the shiny surface of the opposite wall. He smiled, and Megan laughed and waved at him before disappearing into its silvery depths.

Another form was moving towards him, shimmering like a distant star. It was Megan again, but this time a young woman. She placed her hand against the surface as if she were outside looking in through a glass darkly. He placed his hand over hers, and she smiled, nodded briefly, and walked away.

He exited the lift and crossed the lobby, pausing to look at the tree as if seeing its beauty for the first time. Scrooge stood atop the steps and gazed out at the city he loved; the city filled this night with countless hopes and fears. A flake of consecrated snow fell from the heavens, brushing against his lips. He opened his eyes.

Scrooge did not know where Stephen was in the vast, teeming metropolis spread before him, but it did not matter. A light would guide him; he needed only trust and follow. He descended the marble steps into the embrace of the bustling, holy night.

The taxi was waiting for him at the bottom of the stairs, as he knew it would be. The driver got out and watched him ascend the marble stairs. As soon as his feet touched the sidewalk, the cabbie opened the door, and Scrooge got in. No words were exchanged as the taxi drove off into the night.

Somewhere in Central Park, Christmas Morning

A group of men huddled together around a makeshift bonfire. The cracked strains of 'Silent Night' drift upward and, like the smoke, are lost in the bitter night air. Despite their circumstances, they appear happy and content in each other's company. On a park drive, some distance behind them, a taxi pulled up.

The taxi driver opened the door, and Scrooge stepped out. The cabbie pointed in the direction of the small group, and Scrooge began walking towards them. He was not dressed for walking in the snow, and soon his shoes and socks were sodden and cold, but Scrooge did not seem to notice.

As Scrooge drew near, the men became aware of his presence and stopped singing.

One of the men detached himself from the group and moved towards him. They both stopped and faced each other as the snow swirled about them. After a few moments, Scrooge moved forward and embraced the man warmly.

Initially, the vagrant appeared surprised by the gesture, but after a few moments, he responded in kind. The others watched as they hugged each other like long-lost brothers. Eventually, they both turned back towards the little watchful group.

Scrooge produced a fistful of bills from his pocket and began to hand them out liberally, while Stephen revealed the identity of the benevolent stranger. One of the men stepped forward and saluted.

"Good luck, lieutenant," he said in clipped tones.

Stephen returned his salute and then shook the man's hand warmly with his good arm.

"I'll be back," he responded, his voice thick with emotion.

"You can bet your life on that," echoed Scrooge, "until then Merry Christmas to each and every one of you."

The whole group stood to attention as Scrooge and Stephen trudged arm in arm through the snow to the waiting taxi. They had covered about half the distance when the singing began again.

Leah's House, New York City Suburbs, Christmas Day

The sleek black limousine drew up alongside the modest house that was Leah's home. Grainger stepped out and opened the passenger doors. Scrooge and Eva were the first to step outside.

There was a pause before Stephen stepped out of the car. He was clean-shaven and smartly dressed in casual new clothes. He appeared hesitant and nervous as he stared at the house that was once his home.

The front door opened, and Leah stood in the doorway. Seeing Stephen, her hand flew to her mouth, and she appeared unable to move. Stephen walked rapidly towards her, and it was all the motivation Leah needed. She rushed forward and embraced her son. Scrooge turned to Grainger.

"Thank you, Grainger. Go home and spend the rest of the day with your family. I won't be needing you now."

Grainger looked surprised as he made to get in the car.

"Grainger, wait!" shouted Scrooge.

Grainger's shoulders perceptibly sagged as he dutifully turned round.

"Sir?" he inquired, fearing there would be no roast turkey for him today.

"Take an extra week off," said Scrooge, "with full pay, of course."

Grainger's mouth gaped open.

"Really?" he said.

"Merry Christmas," said Scrooge as a grin spread across Grainger's face.

"Merry Christmas to you too, Mr Scrooge," he responded enthusiastically and hastily clambered into the car before his employer could change his mind.

Eva slipped an arm inside Scrooge's as they watched the limo pull away.

"This new, improved Benny is going to take some getting used to," observed Eva.

She turned toward the house.

"We'd better go inside, I think Leah is waiting for us, you especially."

Scrooge did not move.

"You go ahead," he said, "there's something I must do first. Somewhere I have to go."

Eva raised an eyebrow.

"Aren't you forgetting something?" she pointed out. "You've just dismissed Grainger. Where are you going to find a taxi in the burbs on Christmas Day?"

Eva had hardly finished speaking when a yellow taxicab pulled up at the end of the drive. The cabbie, dressed in a peak cap and wearing shades, stepped out and opened the passenger door. Eva stared in amazement.

"Where on earth did he come from?" she gasped.

"He didn't," replied Scrooge enigmatically.

"What?" replied a confused Eva.

Scrooge leaned forward, held Eva by the shoulders and planted a kiss on her cheek.

"Go inside and tell Leah I won't be long."

"What do I say?" Eva asked.

"Tell her there's somewhere I have to go, something I left behind, unfinished business," he added for Eva's benefit.

"She'll understand."

"Business," repeated Eva sceptically, "can't it wait?"

Scrooge looked at her, and there was a sadness in his eyes.

"Not anymore," he replied.

She smiled, resigned to the fact that he would not be swayed.

"It's not what you think, Eva," he said.

Before she had the chance to respond, he took her in his arms and kissed her passionately on the lips.

"I'll be back real soon," he said.

"You'd better be Benny; this is our first date, remember."

She watched him walk down the drive and get into the taxi.

No words were exchanged with the driver who'd stood there the whole time, like a silent sentinel. He shut the door behind Scrooge, and Eva had the impression he already knew their destination.

She watched until the taxi was no longer in sight and made her way to the house.

Outside a Derelict State Orphanage, New York State.

It was boarded up now, had been for years—a building with so many secrets that needed to be exorcised forever. No one visits this district anymore. There was nothing here for anyone, except memories best left undisturbed, like the layers of dust and abandoned cobwebs.

A taxi stopped across the street, and a man looked out of the window. Scrooge studied the bleak building that had shaped and twisted his life. The place was filled with ghosts he had no desire to encounter again. What had he expected to find? This was a mistake. Why had he been brought here?

"You need to get out," said his guide.

"What's the point?" Scrooge protested, "There's nothing here for me anymore. This was a mistake."

The cabbie did not reply; he just stared straight ahead as though he had not heard.

Scrooge knew he had no choice. He stepped out of the taxi onto the sidewalk and felt his shoes crunch and sink into a thick carpet of snow. He turned up his collar against the falling flakes and stared at the orphanage that no longer appeared derelict and abandoned.

The building was just as he remembered it the day he left.

The windows were no longer boarded; instead, they stared down at him in uniform rows, bearing sad, silent witness.

There was one he studied with special interest. He knew every wretched inch of the room that lay beyond, the rose-patterned wallpaper, and the hard little bed next to the tiny dressing table. He remembered how the stairs would creak and groan when someone climbed them.

He was about to turn away as memories threatened to overwhelm him when a face appeared at the window.

The child's eyes widened as he gazed at Scrooge, not across a street, but across a bridge of wasted years. He understood now why he had been compelled to come; what it was he had left behind, what he needed to make him whole again.

He smiled, and the boy smiled back. After everything he had experienced this last night, nothing seemed impossible, so he held out his arms towards the child in the window.

The child backed away, as he had countless times before, but this time he was sure the boy would not curl up, helpless, on the hard little bed.

He waited, watching his breath cloud and dissipate, while time fell about his feet like the snow.

At last, the doors opened, and the child stood on the threshold, an expression of wonder lighting his face. Scrooge took a step forward, almost afraid to move in case the vision dissolved in the cold air, like his silvery breath. His feet sank into fresh snow, and still the child gazed at him.

Scrooge could feel the doubt in the child's heart like a hard stone, and taste the bitter bile of rejection in his mouth. Scrooge knelt on one knee, ignoring the biting wetness, and held out his arms to the boy.

A smile spread across the child's face, and without taking his eyes off Scrooge, he skipped down the steps. His leading foot was planted on the sidewalk when the doors burst open, and Ezekiel Izzard stood on the top step, his face aflame with righteous indignation.

"Ebenezer, get back in here!" he commanded the child.

The boy took a hesitant step forward, looking all the while to Scrooge for reassurance. Scrooge could offer none. A dark familiar shadow had fallen across his soul, and he was one with the child again, numbed by fear and shame.

Izzard descended the steps, nearly slipping on the fresh snow. He grasped the boy by the shoulders, and Scrooge recoiled from his touch. Words recently spoken echoed in his mind like distant thunder.

". . . we couldn't have been that bad. Else you would have left us long ago."

"What are you talking about? I did leave."

"Did you, Ebenezer? Did you really?"

"You're both dead!" he heard himself declare.

"But not to you, Sonny, not to you."

Purifying anger surged through his being, sweeping all before it.

"Let him go, Izzard, you monster!"

Scrooge hurled his words at Ezekiel Izzard like avenging spears. Izzard turned to face him, his hands clawing the boy's shoulders.

"Who are you?" he demanded, but the words no longer held their former power.

"Who are you?" he repeated as though confronted by an accusing spectre who stood just beyond the threshold of his consciousness.

"You know who I am, Ezekiel," said Scrooge, "you cannot hold me any longer."

Izzard looked down at the child and across at Scrooge, and his eyes widened in recognition and disbelief. His grip loosened, and the child scampered free towards Scrooge.

Scrooge lifted the child high above his head, then lowered him slowly. They embraced, and as Izzard watched in horror, the child was absorbed into Scrooge's being until they merged into one.

Ezekiel Izzard opened his mouth to speak, but instead his lips twisted to one side, and he collapsed onto one knee, clawing at his face. Without uttering another word, he fell face down in the snow.

A scream rang out from inside the building, and Stryker appeared on the steps. She hurried towards the fallen form of

Ezekiel Izzard, now covered in fallen snow, and knelt beside him, weeping uncontrollably.

Scrooge did not look back. His guide was waiting beside the open door of the taxi, and a reborn Scrooge stepped inside. He leaned against the plush upholstery and gazed out. The windows of the orphanage were boarded up, and the street was empty and desolate. The dust of Stryker and Izzard blown away on the winds of corruption.

"Where to Ebenezer?" asked the taxi driver."

"Take us home," he replied.

END

CHAPTER 23

THE RED LADY

As they climbed the stairs Billy hung back. He had decided to keep an eye out for the beautiful lady in the red dress. Why had she wanted him to follow her? Perhaps this was part of the trip, and that's why Mr Groucutt had sent him back to get the worksheets. No, that couldn't be it. Mr Groucutt had stopped him following the lady. There must be another reason but whatever it was Billy had most likely missed his chance of ever finding out.

The house was big, but the rooms were dimly lit with wood panelled walls stained dark with age. They reminded Billy of the wood in Uncle Arthur's coffin. Arthur wasn't Billy's real Uncle. He was a resident of The Hollies, and Nan's best friend. After he died Nan wasn't quite the same for a long time. The windows in every room were narrow and let in very little light so people used candles, even in the daytime. Selwyn told them that wood was plentiful from the surrounding forests, which made Billy think he didn't get out much anymore. Selwyn also explained that fire was their greatest fear because so much wood had been used in building the manor. The house smelt musty and unwanted. Nan had begun to smell like that. Like she didn't care any more. The last time he visited her she told him he was the only light left in her life. Billy hadn't understood, but now, in this gloomy room, he thought he knew what she meant.

"This smell's making me feel sick," moaned Brooklyn.

"Why is it so dark?" piped in Kayleigh Williams.

Kayleigh was afraid of the dark. Kayleigh was afraid of everything.

"Dark, Maistress?" Selwyn sounded surprised. "The Manor hath many windows, though glass be a great expense."

"My house has got triple glazing," said Emlyn Gregory, "and we're having solar panels in the roof."

"I know not what marvellous doings ye speak of?" said Selwyn scratching his head. "Come hither, I will show ye something wondrous."

Selwyn was as good as his word. The next room he took them to contained the largest bed Billy had ever seen. There were four wooden pillars on each corner that supported a wooden roof. Curtains were hung around the bed and when they were closed it made a pretty, cool tent.

"Why are there curtains around the bed?" inquired a nervous Melanie Pritchard.

Before Selwyn could answer Rhys Rowlands beat him too it.

"So, they can hide from all the ghosts and vampires and stuff," he said fixing Melanie with wide bug eyes.

"Sir, can we go to the shop now," blurted Kayleigh Williams, near to panic.

"Do not fear young Maistresses. No evil creature would dare enter the manor. We be all God-fearing Baptist folk."

Melanie and Kayleigh did not look convinced. They soon cheered up when they entered the next room. All thoughts of ghosts and vampires faded as they gazed upon the array of clothes spread out on trestles before them. The boys' eyes lit up at the sight of armour and weapons. Mr Groucutt was quick to restrain the more enthusiastic among them.

"Wait a minute! Form an," he paused his face a mask of strained concentration. "Get thee into an orderly, um, queue forthwith."

Billy stood by the door. Much as he wanted to try on the armour, he wanted even more to catch another glimpse of the Red Lady. He watched as Spencer Coombs was fitted with a huge breast plate that touched his knees. There were giggles as he staggered under its weight, and when Selwyn placed the helmet on Spencer's head even Mr Groucutt broke into a laugh.

"I can't see nothing," shouted Spencer.

He sounded as if he were down the bottom of a deep well.

"Stop it Spence," pleaded Ross Tudor, "I'm going to pee myself!"

Selwyn showed no mercy to either boy as he handed Spencer a huge pike. Its long shaft was made of wood and its iron head was a sort of spear and axe welded together. It proved the straw that broke Spencer's back. Without warning Spencer toppled forward dropping the pike in the process. The children scattered screaming as they attempted to avoid being impaled by the falling weapon. Billy was forced to step back onto the landing and that was when he saw the Red Lady again.

At least Billy assumed it was her. The landing extended a long way on either side of the balcony. So far in fact that the ends were as murky as a pond disturbed by careless feet. Near the far end of the landing, they had yet to visit, Billy thought he caught sight of a red silk dress disappearing into one of the rooms. What should he do? The Red Lady had called to him before so she must want him for something. No one would miss him. They were too busy digging Spencer out of his armour. Half expecting Mr Groucutt to roar at him any minute, he dodged the shadows and made his way down the landing.

The last door on the right was slightly ajar. Light peeped through the gap. Someone was inside. He tapped on the door lightly.

"Enter!" came a woman's voice. Billy knew it must be her.

Taking a deep breath, he entered.

She was standing beneath a large portrait with her back to him. The portrait was of a family. Billy guessed the man in the picture must be Colonel Roderick. He stood next to a young woman who was seated. Billy guessed she must be Lady Roderick. Two girls of about three and seven stood directly in front of the Colonel. In a wooden crib by Lady Roderick's feet a baby lay fast asleep. Billy felt sad as he looked at the faces of the children they had lost. Colonel Roderick had long dark hair and a beard. His clothes were silk but not brightly coloured except for the sleeves and collars of his jacket. The collars were large and white while his sleeves seemed to be slashed to allow white silk to peek through. His trousers were of the same material and colour as his jacket bunched at the knees, like Selwyn's. Billy could not help thinking he had seen him somewhere before.

"Was he not a comely man?" said the Red Lady as she turned to face Billy.

For a moment Billy could not speak. She was very beautiful, her dark blue eyes the colour of the violets Nan loved so much. Auburn hair hung in ringlets about her bare white shoulders. But it was not her beauty alone that struck Billy dumb. Although the lady in the portrait wore a blue dress there was no hiding the fact that she and the woman who now stood before him could have been twins.

"I hast not seen thee before, what is thy name?" she asked.

"Billy," was all he could manage.

"Ye are newly appointed to this household? Pray tell, what are thy duties?"

As she spoke Billy noticed that the rims of her eyelids were red and sore. He did not know what she meant by 'duties' but he supposed it didn't really matter as she was only an actress. Emlyn had explained it all to him on the bus. It was really clever though how they picked one that looked just like the real Lady Roderick. Still, it was only polite to answer.

"I've got a paper round," he explained.

The lady looked puzzled. She was as good as those actresses on the tele any day.

"Thy tongue and thy garments are strange to me. No matter. Can I trust thee child?"

She drew closer and knelt before him placing two hands on his shoulders. Billy blushed and nodded.

"This day evil tidings hath come to this house."

She paused and bowed her head. Her shoulders shook and Billy knew she was pretending to cry again. He had to admit she was good but maybe she was overdoing it a bit. After what seemed like ages, she raised her head. Her face was streaked with tears. It was clever how she did that. Perhaps she had a raw onion tucked up her sleeve like magicians did with handkerchiefs. She stood and Billy could see that she did have something in her hand only it wasn't an onion but a large envelope.

"Take this I pray thee and give it to my Land Agent. Hast, thou met him yet?" Her eyes bore into Billy.

"Selwyn you mean?" said Billy wanting to make sure he got it right so Mr Groucutt wouldn't yell at him.

"Selwyn? I know not any Selwyn," she sounded annoyed like Mum whenever Billy brought the wrong thing back from the shop. "I speak of Robert Courtney. He is one I trusted, to my cost," she sighed. "Twas after his coming the shadow fell upon us."

Billy was about to protest that he hadn't met anyone called Robert, but this was just acting after all, so it didn't really matter. Besides he didn't like it when the Red Lady got cross even if it was only pretend.

"Make haste child," said the Red Lady.

He held out his hand and took the envelope. It was heavy. The paper was thick and felt rough to the touch unlike the smooth paper in the school exercise books. In the centre of the envelope was a great blob of red wax that had been pressed down with something. It made a picture, but Billy couldn't quite make out what it was. It smelt of candle wax.

"Conceal it on thy person," commanded the Red Lady.

Billy wasn't sure he liked this part of the trip. He slipped out of his rucksack and hid the letter inside while the Red Lady watched his every move through red rimmed eyes.

"Now child, get thee hence. I would be alone."

The Red Lady's eyes wandered to the far corner of the room, and Billy noticed for the first time a staircase that must lead up to somewhere near the roof.

Billy closed the solid oak door behind him. He could still hear her sobs echoing down the passageway. She's brilliant at her job he thought as he hurried back up the landing. As bad luck would have it, Mr Groucutt stepped out of the room with the armour before Billy had got even halfway back. Mr Groucutt's eyes narrowed as he spied Billy. Billy stopped dead in his tracks. Mr Groucutt was having a bad day and Billy had stepped right into the line of fire. Billy smiled, but it probably came out a stupid grin because Mr Groucutt clenched his teeth. If Mr Groucutt had been taller, with more hair, better looking, and a lot younger, he would have been the spit of that cowboy, Clint something.

"Billy Jenkins! Where have you been this time, boy?"

Maybe it was Billy's imagination, but Mr Groucutt even sounded like the cowboy.

"The lady wanted me sir."

"What lady?" Mr Groucutt's eyes were mere slits.

"The Red Lady."

It was the truth, it just didn't sound it.

"The Red Lady," repeated Mr Groucutt, "and where is this Red Lady?"

Billy pointed back down to the far end of the landing. He didn't take his eyes off Mr Groucutt in case he had to move quickly before Mr Groucutt could grab his ear and give it a sharp tweak. The look on Mr Groucutt's face made Billy worry that his ears weren't the only part of his anatomy under serious threat.

"Perhaps you had better introduce me to this Red Lady of yours."

Although Mr Groucutt smiled his eyes remained threatening black slits. Billy heaved a sigh of relief. Mr Groucutt must be acting too. This was all a part of the trip even if it hadn't been on the itinerary. Taking Mr Groucutt at his word Billy began to make his way back down the corridor. He could hear the heavy tread of footsteps and the creaking of floorboards as Mr Groucutt followed close behind.

"Where goest thou?" Selwyn's voice echoed off the timber panelled walls.

Billy felt Mr Groucutt's hand on his shoulder. Mr Groucutt took a deep breath and exhaled slowly, always a warning sign.

Selwyn was standing in the corridor with a small group of curious children huddled together behind him. From the room could be heard the clanging of metal and the excited voices of his classmates. Billy noticed that the girl next to Selwyn was wearing a dress like one of the children in the portrait. It was Kayleigh Williams. She would have a fit if she knew who it belonged to.

"We goest to see the Red Lady," replied Mr Groucutt.

Billy could hear Mr Groucutt's teeth grinding together.

"Red Lady? If it be Mistress Roderick, you seek you will not find her yonder."

Mr Groucutt gripped Billy's shoulder so tightly his knuckles turned white.

"Why doth that not surprise me?" he said.

Billy wrenched himself free.

"She's down there in the last room. She's been crying. She gave me a letter. Honest!"

More children were spilling onto the landing to see what the fuss was about.

"Come, I will show thee," said Selwyn.

Selwyn stepped forward followed by Billy and Mr Groucutt with the rest of the class in hot pursuit.

"Billy's seen a ghost," whispered Ross Tudor.

A girl whimpered. Selwyn stopped outside the room where the Red Lady was. She didn't seem to be crying any more. He produced a large iron key from somewhere and unlocked the door. Mr Groucutt stepped inside. Billy held his breath.

"Jenkins, get in here boy."

Billy knew he was in deep trouble. Mr Groucutt had given up on the strange language. Billy stepped inside. There was no portrait hanging from the wall and no sign of the Red Lady. No sign of anyone. The room was completely bare.

"But she was in here. She spoke to me. Maybe she's gone up those stairs." The words stumbled off Billy's tongue. His heart sank as he realised that even if the Red Lady had climbed the staircase, she could hardly have taken the portrait and the furniture with her. Had he imagined it all? No, he had proof. There was the letter.

"The stairs have been sealed, young Maister. The Mistress be with her sister whilst the Colonel is away at the wars. Twas once the nursery in happier times. After the cursed Black Death took the children, Colonel Roderick commanded the room henceforth be emptied and shut."

Selwyn's words confused Billy even more. What was going on? How had they managed to clear the room so quickly?

"Billy really have seen a ghost," blurted Ross Tudor, and immediately Kayleigh Williams and Melanie Pritchard started to wail.

"When are we going home sir," blubbed Kayleigh between sobs.

Billy was saved by the appearance of Mistress Selby at the head of the stairs.

"Selwyn," she cried, "fetch these good folk to me, and be quick about it. We have yet to make candles and the day is shortening."